Who will be the next to die?

Terrified, not knowing what was taking place, I dropped to the floor, trying to roll into a ball. I heard someone scream, but it wasn't me. I was making little whimpering noises to myself, wishing I were home, desperately wanting to be off this horrible island and back with my parents.

I heard running footsteps, and what sounded like people bumping and slamming into things. Voices were shouting "Where are the matches?" "Light the candles!" "What happened?" Then Aunt Madelyn, practically next to my ear, screamed, "Andrea!"

I opened my eyes and looked directly into the wide-open, sightless eyes of Judge Arlington-Hughes, whose bloodless face was just inches away from mine.

THE ISLAND OF DANGEROUS DREAMS

Joan Lowery Nixon

Published by
Dell Publishing
a division of
Bantam Doubleday Dell Publishing Group, Inc.
1540 Broadway
New York, New York 10036

The trademark Laurel-Leaf Library® is registered in the U.S. Patent
and Trademark Office.

The trademark Dell® is registered in the U.S. Patent and Trademark
Office.

ISBN: 0-440-20258-2

RL:5.8

Printed in the United States of America

One Previous Edition

August 1992

10 9 8 7 6

RAD

For Martha Farrington,
whose *Murder by the Book* is a happy little island
of dangerous dreams

CHAPTER

~~~~~~~~~~~~~~~~~~~~~~~~

1

I strongly objected to spending a whole month of my summer vacation with Aunt Madelyn. Madelyn scared me.

She was Mom's sister, but she wasn't the least bit like Mom, who was—well, Mom. Mom had the same red hair that her parents had and that I inherited, complete with freckles. On all the charts she would have been checked off as average, except for ten pounds she constantly kept trying to lose. But Madelyn Forbes, in her designer clothes, was tall and very thin with sleek, black hair, narrow red lips, and deep-set eyes. When I was little I thought she was the wicked queen in Disney's *Snow White*.

When I grew a little older and discovered Irish folk tales, I became certain that Madelyn was a changeling, left in the real baby's cradle by evil faeries. Finally, more sophisticated in my knowledge of the world, I decided that the hospital had mixed up records and sent the wrong baby home with Grandma.

Each time I shared my observations with Mom she'd try to explain. "Madelyn is basically a lonely person. She has—well—a little trouble in her relationships with people. She has problems, Andy. Try to understand her."

Now, as I faced Mom across the kitchen table, I said, "Aunt Madelyn scares me, Mom. She's—well, she's creepy."

"Nonsense!" Mom sighed and gazed upward, as though the proper answers for me were pasted on the ceiling.

"Yes, she is too." I tried to make my point. "I still remember when she was here two years ago. She was gloating about some art object that she wanted for that private museum she works for. She said she would have killed to get it, and she chuckled like a mad fiend."

"Andrea," Mom warned. "Don't get so dramatic that you embroider the truth."

"Okay, okay," I said. "She did say that, but the point is that while Madelyn was telling us about this art object her eyes got strange and slanty and glittered like those deep blue marbles underwater in the bottom of your fish bowl, and she gasped a lot while she talked, and her fingers dug into the arms of her chair. And that was creepy."

Mom sighed. "Must you exaggerate like that?"

"I'm not exaggerating. I'm telling what happened." I paused. "Don't blame me. Blame heredity."

Mom blinked. "For what?"

"For the way I describe things. The Irish are great storytellers."

Mom tried so hard not to laugh that she pursed her lips and rubbed her chin. Finally she said, "Listen, Andy, I mean it. You've got things out of proportion. I remember the time you're talking about. Madelyn was merely excited about her purchase, that's all."

I rolled my eyes. "Excited? The understatement of the year. I forgot to say she salivated too."

This time Mom gave up the fight and laughed. She reached across the kitchen table to beat me to the last chocolate cookie in the package. "When are you going to grow up?" she asked.

"I am grown up. I'm seventeen. I'm old enough to get a job this summer, not go to Palm Beach to visit Aunt Madelyn."

Mom gulped down the last crumb of cookie and her eyes became serious. "If you're so grown up," she said, "then let's discuss this situation as two adults would. Your father and I are trying to—to work out a problem."

I nodded, only too unhappily familiar with the frosty silences between them that caught me in the same draft. My dad's a great guy, so good at working out personnel problems for his Houston company that his boss uses him overtime as a troubleshooter. Mom is probably one of the best student counselors in the nearby Bayport school district, known for getting a lot of kids back on their feet and headed in the right direction. They understand people so well. They just couldn't seem to understand each other.

It's awful to think that your parents might split up. At night I'd pull the blanket over my head, as though that would shut out all the unhappiness in our house, and try to pretend that all the smiles and hugs were back in place, but it didn't work. I'd read the magazine articles that say kids unfairly blame themselves when their parents' marriages break up, but even so the guilt was heavier than my blanket, and I'd ask myself over and over, "Did I do something wrong? Was it my fault?" There wasn't anyone to answer.

Mom and Dad weren't the only ones who were having problems. My throat tightened, and it hurt to swallow, as I thought of the differences I had had with Rick, differences that became arguments, arguments that had suddenly turned into a final good-bye.

"You have to learn to roll with the punches," Rick grumbled at me. "The world isn't fair, and part of growing up is accepting that fact. You're too intense. You take on a cause and don't let go. Sometimes you drive me crazy."

"But if something is wrong—"

"Then let someone else handle it for a change. Like that thing with Mrs. What's-her-name in the library."

"She's not Mrs. What's-her-name!" I shouted at him. "She's Mrs. Lankersham! And she's worked as a library aide ever since I was a little kid, and now the mayor wants to make more library cuts and kick her and the other aides out, and—"

"Spare me," Rick said. He gave a long sigh and I could see him deliberate, then change tactics. He smiled. "Andy, that civic meeting is the same night as the BeeJay dance."

I just nodded.

"So make a choice," he said.

"I don't have a choice," I whispered, hoping with all my heart that he'd understand and knowing he wouldn't. "Mrs. Lankersham has been a friend almost all my life. I can't let her down. I promised that—"

"You made some promises to me too."

"But—"

"I told you. Make a choice."

I shivered, not just because I was hurt. Anger began as a hot, tight lump in my chest and exploded into sharp, red flashes. No one had the right to back me against a wall—not even Rick. "Then I choose Mrs. Lankersham," I snapped.

I don't think I really expected Rick to give in. I was just reacting, not thinking at all. Rick isn't the only one who tells me that I'm stubborn. Mom has said it too. But I couldn't help my decision. I couldn't desert Mrs. Lankersham.

Rick stuck his hands in his pockets and stared down at the ground for a few minutes. When he looked up he had a strangely calm expression on his face. "I guess this is it, Andy," he said.

Now I was scared. "What do you mean?" I asked him. I knew darned well what he meant, but I couldn't believe it.

"Look, we've had a lot of fun together. I guess we really cared a lot about each other for a while—"

I grabbed his arm, interrupting. "But I do care! I love you!"

"Not enough," he said.

"How about you?" I whispered. "I thought you cared about me."

He shook his head and stepped away from me. "It's over, Andy."

"No! Rick, if you could just try to understand about Mrs. Lankersham—"

"It's not just the Mrs. Lankersham thing. It's— well, it's just time for both of us to move on."

"I don't believe it," I insisted. "I won't!"

"You're making this tougher than it needs to be."

I could feel the tears on my cheeks, but I didn't try to brush them away. *"I'm* making it tough?" I shouted at him. "Don't try to blame *me*!"

Rick just shrugged. "Grow up, Andy," he said.

I watched him walk away. I would never forget that moment.

"Andy." Mom laid her hand on mine, jolting me back to the present. "I also thought that you might like to get away from Bayport for a while." She added hesitantly, "Now that you and Rick aren't dating any longer."

"That sounds too final," I said quickly, her words making everything even worse. "Maybe . . ."

I stopped, and Mom tried a tentative smile. "Honey, you have to face facts. Rick's dating another girl. It's time for you to go out with other boys."

"I don't want to. It wouldn't be any fun."

"You're only seventeen, Andy, and Rick was just a first love."

I stubbornly shook my head, but she didn't stop.

"You have to let go," Mom said.

I folded my arms tightly across my chest and said, "I don't want to talk about Rick."

"Okay," Mom answered. "Then let's talk about your father and me. We're honestly trying to work out our problems, and I know that we will, given a little quiet time together."

They wanted me out of the way, while at the same time I wanted to cling to them. I tried to hide the pain and keep it light. "Get rid of the kid," I said. "Send her to the movies. Ship her off to camp. Sell her to the gypsies."

"Andrea!"

I winced at the hurt in her eyes. "Take it easy, Mom," I said. "You've heard of 'laughing to keep from crying.' I'm trying to tell you that I want things to work out too. Of course I'll help. I'll go to visit Aunt Madelyn."

"Thank you," Mom said.

"Will Madelyn?"

"Will Madelyn what?"

"Thank me for coming? I can't imagine her wanting to have me as a houseguest for a whole month."

However, Madelyn wrote a lovely, gracious letter of invitation in a backhand script as elegant as her thick, cream-colored stationery. I accepted on a sheet from a speckled-gray, recycled notepad that was the only paper I could find in the house.

More than a dozen times during the next few

days I stood by the telephone, staring at it. Maybe if I called Rick, maybe if he heard my voice . . .

"Don't go, Andy," he'd say. "I've missed you. I want to see you again. Now."

Once I even picked up the receiver and dialed the first three digits of his phone number. But I couldn't go through with it. I'd call when I came back. That would be a good time to work things out. Not now, but after I came home again. If Mom and Dad could solve their problems—and they would, they had to!—then why couldn't Rick and I?

While I packed my shorts, T-shirts, and jeans, I tried to keep from thinking about Rick and zeroed in on positive thoughts about visiting Madelyn. Palm Beach was practically next door to Disney World and not very far from the Everglades and Cypress Gardens and all sorts of neat touristy stuff. Surely Aunt Madelyn would want to entertain her one and only niece by going with me to all these places. Wouldn't she?

It didn't take long after I arrived in Palm Beach to find out that she wouldn't.

"This is a golden opportunity for you to broaden your horizons," Madelyn informed me. "We'll give you a good introduction to the world of art."

"I know something about art," I told her. "Last summer I did some volunteer work at our Bayport science museum, and the museum chairman, Dr. Sammy Kirschman, was a real nut on South American artifacts."

"A 'real nut on artifacts'?" Madelyn mimicked. "I do believe, Andrea, that there is a great deal more about art for you to discover." Aunt Madelyn looked at me as though she'd been handed a hopeless case, and we set off in her little white BMW for a tour of her favorite art museum—the Sartington, where she was curator. It was the first art museum of many.

I have nothing against art museums. In fact, I really like art museums. Mom and I often go to the Houston Museum of Fine Art when we're in the city, and once, on vacation, Dad, Mom, and I spent a whole, wonderful day in the big Art Institute in Chicago. We saw what we wanted to and skipped the exhibits we didn't like, and nobody at either place asked questions to see if I was paying attention.

On my fourth day in Palm Beach, Madelyn and I drove down the coast to visit a museum where Aunt Madelyn had an appointment with the curator. She left me in the South and Central American room among the squatty clay figures and broken pots.

"You'll enjoy this display, since you have a smattering of information on artifacts," she said. "The museum has a few excellent pieces of hammered-gold jewelry from the Mayan period that will fascinate you. We'll discuss them when I get back."

I hated to admit to myself that Aunt Madelyn could be right, but when I found the case containing the gold jewelry and stared inside, my eyes widened with surprise. It wasn't the same kind of gold that was in Mom's wedding ring or Dad's wristwatch. It was a deeper yellow and looked softer and more pliable. There were crude marks from what must have been some kind of mallet, but at the same time there was a delicate intricacy in the designs.

A guard sauntered into the room and stood nearby.

I looked up at him and smiled.

"Beautiful, aren't they?" he said.

"Yes," I answered, "but they don't belong here."

He stretched his neck to glance into the case, as though we weren't talking about the same thing. "Sure, they do." His voice was puzzled. "They're the property of the museum."

I shook my head. "They're really the property of the country of Mexico."

"Naw," he said, while he studied me to see if I was joking. "The museum owns all this stuff in here."

"It was stolen," I told him, and proceeded to fill him in on everything Dr. Kirschman had told us about how countries desperately try to hang on to their artifacts, but looters steal them from archaeological digs and sell them to people who smuggle them into the United States to brokers. Then brokers here sell the artifacts to certain art dealers, who in turn sell them to wealthy art collectors anywhere in the world. I even told him what Dr. Kirschman said about some collectors paying so much money that a lot of crooks who specialize in art theft had gotten into the act.

The guard blinked a couple of times after I finished and said, "Are you trying to tell me that this museum is dealing in stolen artifacts?"

"No," I said. I bent to peer at the card in the

corner of the case. "These pieces were donated. But the person who donated them knew they were stolen."

He looked puzzled and shrugged. "Does it make any difference how or why the artifacts got here?"

"Of course it does," I said. "It does to me. It should to everybody. Stealing is stealing, whether it's from somebody's house or somebody's country."

Aunt Madelyn walked toward us so quickly that her high heels on the marble floor click-clacked as fast as typewriter keys. "Andrea," she said, "I've had an important phone call. We've got to get back to my office."

As we hurried out I looked back at the guard, who was bent over, scowling at the contents of the glass case filled with Mayan gold.

Aunt Madelyn drove too fast and kept drumming her fingertips on the steering wheel. I think she forgot I was seated next to her, because a couple of times she mumbled something to herself.

It made me nervous. Just a few more miles per hour and we probably would get a good aerial view of the highway. I knew she hadn't filed a flight plan. I decided to break into her private world of race-car driving by saying something subtle, so I blurted out, "That must have been some telephone message!"

Aunt Madelyn's lips parted in surprise and she gave me a quick glance, swerving into the next lane and near-missing a camper truck. In return the driver tried to damage our eardrums with a long blast on his horn.

The combination must have worked. Aunt Madelyn's right foot eased up on the accelerator and she leaned back against the seat, taking a long breath. "The phone message," she repeated. "Oh, yes. The call was from a friend of mine."

"Urgent?"

"Moderately so."

I wasn't going to figure that one out. "A male friend," I decided aloud.

"A *business* friend, Judge Justin Arlington-Hughes," Madelyn said, with the same hungry eagerness that she had used in the restaurant last night when she'd ordered a lobster soufflé. "I think he called because . . ."

She stopped, so I asked, "Because why?"

Madelyn shrugged. "I'm not going to second-guess."

"Good idea," I said in an attempt to keep the conversation rolling, but she slipped me one of those narrow-eyed, probing glances, as though she thought I was trying to be funny, and stopped talking to me. I used the time to think about Rick. I missed him terribly. Mom was wrong in telling me I had to let go. She didn't understand how much I cared about Rick.

It didn't take long to get back to Palm Beach and to the Sartington Museum, which was an elegant one-storied, gleaming-white building set like a centerpiece in its own little park of tropical yellow calla lilies, scarlet salvia, and gaudy purslane. We entered the carved doors of the museum under an arch of bougainvillaea that dripped clusters of dark red blossoms. The blond woman at the desk in the entry hall looked up and smiled, as did the guard, who actually touched the brim of his cap to Aunt Madelyn.

The entry hall to the museum was an intimidating expanse of cool white marble. In the center of the hall stood a pedestal, upon which was a curled stone something that stared at me with one large blank eye. I got out of its line of vision by trotting after Madelyn into her nearby office.

It didn't help. Dominating her office was a painting of two flat, purple people with double profiles, their tongues hanging out, and large round holes through their chests. They stared at me too. Pointedly ignoring them and hoping they'd get the hint, I dropped into a chair and thumbed through a magazine—art magazine, of course—while Madelyn called her friend, the judge. Finally she hung up the receiver and hurried around the desk. I jumped to my feet.

Madelyn clutched my shoulders, holding me at arm's length and grinning so broadly that her face scrunched into a grimace. I could feel energy vibrating through her fingertips like a burst of electricity.

"I can't believe it!" she said. "I can't!"

"Believe what?" I tried to wiggle away from her hold.

Her smile crinkled again, making little cracks in her makeup. "I'll get to that later," she said. "First, I can tell you that Judge Arlington-Hughes has extended an invitation to spend the weekend at his home in the Bahamas."

This caught my attention fast. I'd seen pictures

of those white sand beaches! "It's nice of him to help you entertain me."

"He doesn't exactly know about you yet," she said, "but there's no reason why you shouldn't be included."

She seemed very sure, so I didn't worry about it. "Is his house near Nassau?"

Madelyn shook her head. "No. It's not really far from the coast of Florida. The judge owns a small island in the Little Bahama Banks."

"A whole island? Wow!"

Madelyn stepped back and smiled a catlike, secret smile. "Now, for the big news. I want you to keep this information to yourself, Andrea. This invitation was not given for purely social reasons. Justin has come into possession of a glorious Peruvian artifact and will show it to me there. I know he'll give the Sartington first chance to purchase it."

"Where did the artifact come from?" I asked her.

She blinked and, as though she were speaking to someone who wasn't all there, said slowly, "From Peru, Andrea. I told you that."

"I mean, has the artifact been in this country for a long time, or was it just smuggled in from Peru?"

She just stared at me, so I went on. "I wish you could meet Dr. Kirschman," I added. "He's the most terrific science teacher. You'd like him. Everybody likes him. Anyhow, last summer Dr. Kirschman told us that most countries in South and Central America have laws to prevent people from taking artifacts outside their countries, and yet people steal them. Can you believe it? Stealing important parts of a country's past?"

Aunt Madelyn gave me one of those impatient looks that I'd begun getting used to. "My dear girl," she said, "you obviously know nothing about art collecting."

"I know that a lot of the collections owned by wealthy collectors in this country are made up of stolen artifacts," I told her. "And a lot of museums once got their collections in the same way. It isn't right, Aunt Madelyn. It isn't fair."

She made an impatient shooing motion with her right hand. "But it's business," she said.

I was shocked. "Is the artifact stolen?" I asked. "You didn't answer my question."

"Darling Andrea, if you had the vaguest idea of the type of work I do, you would know that there are times it is best *not* to ask questions."

"Your judge friend stole the artifact."

"Of course he didn't! He—he obtained it from someone."

"Who stole it."

"Andrea! I should just leave you here!"

I thought about those clean beaches with the clear, turquoise water I'd seen in photographs and said quickly, "No. I'd rather go with you."

"Then promise you'll keep your opinions to yourself!" Aunt Madelyn said. "This will be a business deal with no room for childish, ignorant, pseudo-moralizing."

One of the purple profiles looked as though it was about to gag. I didn't want to stay and see if it would. "I'll keep quiet," I answered.

"Very well then," she said, still irritated enough to add a miffed sniff. "Go to the ladies' room and comb your hair. We're going to meet Justin for lunch."

"Just one more thing," I said. "There's something I don't understand. Why couldn't the judge show you the artifact here? Why do you have to go to his island? It all sounds weird to me. Urgent telephone calls, secret information, maybe even a boat slipping through the dark water at night—"

"Andrea!" Madelyn snapped. "I told you to comb your hair! No more nonsense!"

But as I left the room I could see the indecision in her eyes. I could guess that I wasn't the only one who had some questions about the judge's actions.

CHAPTER

~~~~~~~~~~~~~~~~~~~~

2

Judge Justin Arlington-Hughes and my aunt matched as well as salt and pepper shakers. They both stood tall, their backbones held up more by pomposity than by devotion to good posture. His mane of white hair contrasted nicely with her sleek, dark hair. His navy-blue suit was impeccable. Her navy-blue suit seemed exactly right for the curator of the Sartington.

The judge looked me over thoroughly, then glowered. I knew what he was thinking. He hadn't planned on including me, and he was trying to figure out how to rework the invitation so that I'd be left out.

Aunt Madelyn, who was studying the menu, didn't seem to notice. I was thankful when the waitress arrived to take our orders and interrupted his scowl.

After we got past the opening conversational trivialities and my aunt's mild embarassment because she and the judge ordered black coffee and

salads, while I scarfed down a burger with everything, double fries, and a large strawberry shake, I
heard enough to make me disgusted with both of
them.

Someone, with whom Judge Arlington-Hughes
had "connections," had smuggled the artifact into
the United States and into the judge's hands by
way of his sizable bank account.

The judge leaned across the table and murmured, "Wait until you see it, Madelyn! It's a rare
find. Gold with an unbelievably large blue topaz.
I've never come across anything like it."

I didn't miss Aunt Madelyn's quick glance in my
direction before she spoke to the judge. I'd been
right. She'd shared some of my suspicions. "Don't
make me wait to see it! Why can't I see it now?"
she coaxed. Her breathing became even more erratic, and I tried to remember what to do for people who are hyperventilating.

The judge leaned back against the booth and
smiled. His words dripped with a smug superior-
ity. "As I told you, you'll see it tomorrow, when we
reach my island."

Aunt Madelyn was so impatient, she almost
snapped at the judge. "You're up to something,
Justin. I know you are."

He grinned and widened his eyes, trying to look
innocent. "I can't imagine what you mean."

She leaned forward. "You are offering this to me
exclusively, aren't you?"

"Would you like another cup of coffee?" he
asked.

She actually slapped the table so hard that the

empty cups jiggled, and I dropped a greasy french fry into my lap. "Ah-ha! You're not answering my question." Madelyn paused and tried a different approach, her voice slipping out like thick cream. "Justin, dear, our friendship should count for something, shouldn't it?"

"Friendship should never be mixed with business," he answered.

For a moment they just stared at each other, their eyes like dark blue laser beams. I wouldn't have been surprised to see smoke rising from little holes in their foreheads. Then the judge said, "Tomorrow, Madelyn, I'll expect you to meet me promptly at ten A.M. at the boat slip in Fort Lauderdale. You know where to find the *Croesus*."

Ten A.M. So much for dark water at night.

"Andrea and I will be there."

"Perhaps there's something else that Andrea might want to do," he offered.

"She's in my care, Justin," Madelyn said. "Of course she'll come. There's plenty of room on your boat for just the three of us, so there's no problem in including Andrea."

He began to speak, then changed his mind. Madelyn's eyes became little slits, and she said, "It won't be just the three of us, will it, Justin? You're bringing someone else! Who?"

He dabbed at his chin with his napkin and said, "Madelyn, you have been invited. Either accept or refuse, as you see fit."

"I wish I had even an inkling of what you are planning," Madelyn said.

"Trust me."

She smiled, but there wasn't any humor in it. "Justin, dear, I'd never be that foolish."

"I'll see you tomorrow," he said. He picked up the check and slid from the booth. Before he walked to the cashier's desk he gave me a smile that could have just been taken from the cafe freezer and said, "It was a pleasure to meet you, Andrea."

I stammered something polite in return, but I didn't mean what I said any more than he did.

Madelyn collected her handbag and prepared to follow, but I reached across the table and grabbed her arm. "Let's not go," I whispered.

"Why in the world not?"

"I don't like the way he's behaving. I don't even like him."

"This is a business proposition, Andrea. Likes and dislikes don't matter."

"But I feel strange about going with him. Creepy. Weird. I know it's just a hunch, but . . ."

She pulled away, slipped gracefully from the booth, and stood over me. "You don't conduct business by following hunches, Andrea."

I got up, too, and followed her out to her car. Once inside, she seemed to relax a little, although the skin over her knuckles was stretched tight as she gripped the wheel. I was surprised at what an intense person she was.

"Maybe I could go home," I said, hoping desperately that she'd agree.

She turned to stare at me for just an instant, her eyes wide. "I thought you were enjoying your visit with me."

"Oh, I am," I said, nearly choking on the words.

"I'm glad," she said, "because it's a pleasure for me to have you here."

With a start I realized that she meant it.

"You're my only niece, and I've always felt close to you." I guess the words sounded odd to her, too, because she gave a funny little laugh and added, "I don't get close to many people, Andrea. Maybe I don't know how to show what I feel. But believe me, I don't want you to go home. I want you to come with me. You'll love the island and the swimming. Justin has a beautiful place."

"I'll be in the way." I almost groaned aloud. No matter where I went I seemed to be in the way.

"No, you won't," Madelyn said. "Just relax and enjoy yourself and leave the business to us." Maybe she felt me studying her, because she smiled and said, "The work that I do is the most important part of my life. Correction. It *is* my life. Do you understand that, Andrea?"

"I don't know," I said. Again I felt strange with Madelyn, a little frightened of her. I didn't want to go to the Bahama island with Madelyn and the judge. I wanted to go home. As soon as I had a chance, I was going to call my mother.

That evening, while Madelyn was doing her gourmet thing in the kitchen of her high-rise apartment, boiling bags of something frozen for our dinner, I dialed our home phone and reversed the charges.

"Sorry," the operator said after the eighth ring. "No answer. Shall I try later?"

"No, thanks," I told her. I didn't want the call to go through at a time when Madelyn could hear what was being said. I'd just wait until I had another good chance.

The good chance didn't come until after we had packed for the weekend, Madelyn had set the alarm for six, and we had gone to bed.

I tiptoed down the hall and back into the kitchen, where I was sure she wouldn't hear me making the call. Eagerly I dialed again. With the time-zone change, Mom and Dad wouldn't be asleep yet. Dad would be listening to the evening news, as he did every night before going to bed. The phone rang and rang until finally the operator went through the "sorry" routine.

"No," I said as I fought back tears. "Don't try again." I hung up the receiver and leaned against the wall, missing my parents with an ache so strong that my chest hurt. Rick hadn't wanted me. The judge didn't want me around. And now my parents had shut me out. I knew I was being unreasonable, but I felt like a little kid who was lost. I didn't know which way to go. What made everything worse was facing the weekend I was going to have to spend with Aunt Madelyn and the judge.

CHAPTER

~~~~~~~~~~~~~~~~~~~

3

Aunt Madelyn had been to the boat slip before, so she found the judge's boat easily. I followed her up the gangplank and back to the canopied stern with its blue cushioned seats in a U shape around the railing. "It's a lovely boat," Madelyn said. Some boat! Calling that elegant, gleaming affair a boat was a gigantic understatement. Its teakwood deck and glossy brass trim sparkled under a clear sky. The air was filled with all the wonderful ocean smells of salt and seaweed, and gulls dipped, cried, and plummeted into the sea, coming up with small fish in their beaks.

I touched the camera that hung around my neck. I'd want to record this to show Mom, Dad, and Rick. They'd never be able to imagine the overall gorgeousness of this fantastic boat unless they could see pictures of it.

I began to perk up until I saw that Madelyn was doing a pretty fair imitation of the wicked queen finding out from the magic mirror that Snow

White was still alive. I whirled to see what she was glowering at and saw a small, trim woman dressed in white slacks and a red-striped shirt who was struggling with an overstuffed overnight bag. Short brown curls poked out from under a yachting cap, which I thought was a pretty hokey touch until I reminded myself that I knew nothing about boats like this and maybe that cap went with the territory.

The woman, who couldn't have been much older than forty, tripped up the gangplank and managed to land on deck, dropping her bag at her feet. She stared at me in bewilderment. "What is this?" she asked. "Have we had a change of plans?"

Aunt Madelyn had regained all her poise and behaved as though she were hostess and had planned the whole trip. "How nice you could come, Benita. May I present my niece, Andrea Ryan? Benita Robley."

"How do you do," Benita said. She turned to Madelyn. "I was under the impression that this weekend was to be a business meeting, but here you are with your niece. Exactly what is this all about?"

Madelyn tried to look wise. "Justin will let you in on his plans when he's ready. You know Justin."

Benita plopped down on the nearest cushioned bench. She seemed to be upset that I was there. Was I going to affect everyone like that? "Bother, Madelyn, I shouldn't have asked you," Benita said. "You don't know any more about this than I do. Where is Justin, anyway?"

"Here I am." The judge, who was dressed like a star from an old movie, in a blue yachting blazer, white slacks, and an ascot, climbed the stairs from the cabin and gave Benita and Madelyn each a kiss on the cheek. He nodded a grudging greeting in my direction.

I didn't want to be on this boat any more than he wanted me here. In my plain yellow T-shirt, blue shorts, and half a bottle of number fifteen sun block, I didn't even belong at this costume party. I wished I could have told him that.

There were footsteps on the galley stairs, and a tall, dark-haired, broad-shouldered guy, who would have looked more at home on a football field than on a boat, appeared behind the judge. The two women knew him, and he was introduced to me as Kurt Cameron, one of the judge's secretaries. That seemed a funny job for a guy that big. I had to wipe away a smile as I pictured him crammed into one of those little secretarial chairs, typing letters for the judge.

Benita threw him a couple of intense looks that I couldn't figure out. Maybe he couldn't either, because he just scowled at her. The judge chatted with Madelyn and ignored me. It was going to be a horrible weekend.

A voice shouted behind me, making me jump, "Ahoy, the *Croesus*!"

"Come aboard," Judge Arlington-Hughes called, and I turned to see a small, fair-skinned man dressed in white duck pants, a blue- and white-striped shirt, blue deck shoes, and a floppy white cotton hat pulled down around his ears. A clear green visor was inserted into the hat brim in front, and he squinted through the visor to study us. He looked like the kind of person who would yell "Hello" at a boat.

A much taller, graying man, who seemed uncomfortably out of place in a sport jacket and slacks, shirt and tie, stepped up behind him.

"Come aboard!" the judge repeated. "Both of you."

The two men stared at each other, first with surprise, then suspicion. The judge tried to suppress a smile, like a kid who was watching someone else get blamed for something he had done.

As soon at the men were on deck the judge introduced the small man as Norton Lindsay. Norton shook his head. "Never mind," he said curtly. "I know everyone here."

But the older man introduced himself as Aldo Malcolm. The judge studied him quizzically, then said, "We must have met before, Mr. Malcolm."

"I don't believe we have," Aldo said.

The judge shook his head. "I have a good memory for faces. Eventually I'll remember where and when I've seen you."

Aldo smiled. "Then you'll have the advantage, because to my knowledge we have never met."

Benita's glance fluttered between Aldo, Kurt, and the judge like a hyperactive butterfly, but Madelyn was poised for the occasion. She held out a cool hand toward Norton Lindsay and said, "So, Norton, you're here to represent Franklin Granakee."

Norton smiled and answered, "As you know, I'm his best agent."

I knew who Franklin Granakee was. Everybody who could read knew about him. He owned an oil company and a bunch of hotels and some other companies and was in the news last year for paying over ten million dollars for a painting for his private collection. But I didn't know what he looked like. He was supposed to be so protective of his privacy that he rarely went out in public and never allowed himself to be photographed.

Norton's appraisal swept across the rest of us. "I seem to have been misinformed. When I was invited I was not told that I would be part of a group."

Judge Arlington-Hughes's secret smile returned as he said, "Please make yourself comfortable, Norton. Who knows? You may find this to be an extremely profitable weekend vacation."

Aunt Madelyn quickly turned from Norton to Aldo Malcolm, who shifted from one foot to the other. He was sweating in that sport jacket. I felt sorry for him and wished he'd at least take off his tie and relax. "Mr. Malcolm," she said, "are you—"

He interrupted. "Aldo, please. You are all on a first-name basis. I don't wish to be different."

"Very well, Aldo," she said, smoothly slipping into what she really wanted to know. "The rest of us are familiar with each other's positions. Benita represents the Gridling Art Auction House, Norton bids for Franklin Granakee, and I represent the Sartington Museum—a private collection open to the public. And you?"

He shrugged, letting us all wait a moment before he answered, "You get directly to the point, don't you?"

"Yes, I do," she said. "Well?"

"Let's just say that I'm here, as you are, to bid for the artifact."

"For yourself?"

"For someone who doesn't wish his name to be known."

"Someone from this country?"

"Does it matter?"

I couldn't stand it. Madelyn and Aldo were playing twenty questions about an artifact that didn't and shouldn't belong to any of them in the first place. So I said, "If we each get a guess about the person Aldo represents, I'd like to be first. I'll say he's a Mideastern sheik who owns a villa in France, a town house in London, an estate in Beverly Hills, and a hotel in New York."

Aunt Madelyn looked ready to throw me overboard, but Aldo smiled. "An amazing guess," he said.

Norton made a noise between a sniff and a snicker, but I stammered, "You mean I'm right?"

Madelyn looked extremely irritated, to put it mildly. "Well," she said, "it certainly wouldn't be the first time Mideastern oil money was involved in an art sale."

They could buy Aldo's statement, but I didn't. He looked so smugly pleased with himself that I wished I hadn't butted in with my ridiculous explanation.

"Enough speculation," Judge Arlington-Hughes

said. "I was satisfied with Mr. Malcolm's credentials when they were presented to me, and that's all that matters. I'm sure you'll agree." The judge elbowed through us and to the front of the boat, where two deckhands had appeared. Ropes were pulled from cleats, and the sailors jumped aboard.

"Be seated. Make yourselves comfortable. We're taking off now," the judge shouted to us, and he climbed some stairs to a small wheelhouse.

I pulled the lens cover off my camera and aimed at the dock, but before I had a chance to snap the picture the camera was firmly pulled downward. "Under the circumstances, there should be no pictures," Aldo said.

"I won't take your picture if you don't want me to," I said. "But I'd like some shots of the boat and the ocean and the island. This is my vacation."

"This may be a vacation for you, but it's a business trip for the rest of us," Norton said. "I agree with Aldo. No photographs."

Aunt Madelyn held out a hand for the camera. "Give it to me, Andrea. I'll keep it for you in my handbag."

I had no choice. I turned over the camera to her, wondering what was with these guys. I suppose I wouldn't want my picture taken if I were dressed like they were. Or if I really did represent a sheik. I was going to have a miserable weekend vacation with these people!

Benita, Madelyn, Norton, Aldo, and I squeezed together on the cushions around the U-shaped railing. Kurt disappeared into the galley and soon came back with some orange juice and cinnamon rolls. It was easy to balance plates and glasses on our knees while we puttered through the harbor, but once out at sea, moving at a fast clip up and down through the swells, it became a close-packed juggling act.

Judge Arlington-Hughes turned the wheel over to one of his deckhands and came to join us. As soon as he had squirmed into position on the bench, casting an impatient glance in my direction, Aunt Madelyn got right to the point again.

"Don't you think it's time now, Justin, to tell us what all this secrecy and mystery are about?"

"Very simple, Madelyn," he said. He took a large bite of a cinnamon roll and leisurely chewed and swallowed it before he continued. By this time he had everyone's attention. "As you know, I am in possession of a particularly valuable Peruvian artifact. Whereas the stones in most South American artifacts are jade or emeralds, this stone happens to be a very large blue topaz. I hope that this topaz will bring me a great deal of money, and that's why each of you happens to be here."

"Am I the only one who didn't know others were to be invited?"

"None of you were told," he said. "That was essential, especially after what happened the last time, when I offered the small Delaroche painting."

No one spoke. Aldo looked puzzled, Benita looked guilty, and Madelyn's lips pressed into a thin, red line. Norton chuckled.

"What happened?" I had to know.

Norton was the only one who answered. "There

was some chicanery involved. Telephone calls were intercepted, misinformation was given. The Sartington ended up with the painting."

"I had nothing to do with that message to your hotel operator that you did not wish to receive calls," Madelyn said.

"It doesn't matter now," Norton said. "In fact, I do believe that someone did me—or, more directly, Mr. Granakee—a favor. I am sure that what was purported to be a Delaroche was not by Delaroche at all, but by a lesser artist, one of his students."

"Impossible!" Madelyn said, and the conversation turned to a short, impassioned discussion of Delaroche's technique.

Kurt collected the empty dishes and carried them down the stairs, disappearing into the galley.

Aldo, who was squashed between Benita and me at the side of the boat deck, smiled at me pleasantly. "I have a daughter who is probably close to your age," he said. "Sixteen? Seventeen?"

"Seventeen," I answered.

"She loves to ski," he said. "Do you ski?"

I shook my head. "Swim. The Texas Gulf Coast has good swimming weather. We'd have to travel quite a distance to get to a ski resort." Trying to keep the conversation going, I asked, "Do you ski with her?"

"Every chance I get," he said, his eyes sparkling. "Elizabeth is a wonderful girl, a perfect daughter."

"Tell me about her," I said.

But Benita's voice rose, interrupting our conversation. "That's enough, Madelyn! Norton!" she said. "You aren't going to get anywhere with that argument. We're wasting time. I want to see the artifact." She tugged at the judge's sleeve. "Come on, Justin. Can't we see it now?"

"Of course not," the judge said. "I wouldn't risk passing it around here at sea. It's safely tucked away in my home on the island."

He managed to lean back and smile. "You'll be able to examine it at your leisure, with no telephones, no tricks, no leaking information to the press."

"It's that important to you?" Madelyn asked.

"Yes," he said. "And there's another reason. Because of the artifact's great value, it's essential that I protect it from theft."

Theft? He was a fine one to talk!

A corner of Norton's mouth twisted down, and he peered upward through his green eyeshade. "The word is out that you have the artifact," he murmured.

Benita pouted. "Justin, I don't think you trust us either. When your secretary investigated us he didn't attempt to hide it."

"On my orders," the judge said. "Both Kurt and I felt it advisable to let you know how thoroughly your backgrounds and connections would be looked into. Kurt did an excellent job on each and every one of you."

But not on me, I thought, wanting to laugh aloud. I could be a spy, an agent for a foreign power, the head of the Mafia, and no one would know it. No one would suspect me. I was just Madelyn's niece, an uninvited, unwanted guest.

Spray stung my cheek as the boat nosed into a high swell, and an idea struck me with the same force. Each of the invited guests on this boat wanted that artifact. But so did I. I wanted it to be returned to the country of Peru.

CHAPTER

~~~~~~~~~~~~~~

4

We were a floating restaurant all the way out to the island. It's a good thing that none of us were inclined toward seasickness. Kurt appeared with a large tray of sandwiches and fruit. When the tray was empty he did a disappearing act and came up this time with assorted cookies. He kept a bar going, and luckily there were plenty of soft drinks.

Benita sipped on a diet cola, simpering a bit as she said she never mixed drinking with business and wanted to keep a clear head for whatever was in store.

"You're going to love Justin's house," she explained to Aldo. "It's an old plantation-style home, with wide verandas on both floors. The rooms on the verandas face the sea, and they have marvelous louvered doors that open wide to the breeze. Absolutely delightful. A gorgeous place to entertain. I'll never forget Justin's birthday party last year. Madelyn and I were there. Norton, too, as I remember."

Norton shook his head emphatically. "I've never been to Justin's island."

"But you must have been," Benita said. "I distinctly remember—"

"Incorrectly," Norton interrupted. "Just ask Justin. This is not only my first trip to his island, it's my first trip to Florida."

"I believe that's right," the judge said.

"But I could almost swear that . . ."

Madelyn smiled. "You're thinking of the Art Gala in Santa Barbara in '85."

Benita sighed. "Well, if you all say so. I honestly don't know how I can get one party so confused with another."

"Perhaps it's your age, dear," Madelyn murmured.

I tuned them out. It was more interesting to watch the horizon, where small, dark blobs began to emerge as islands, looming up around us as we wove our way between them. Here and there I saw a house or two or a small boat, but most of the islands seemed to be uninhabited. We went through stretches of open sea, then islands again, then sea. Finally there was a change in the pitch of the boat's motors and we swung inward, around a wooded promontory at the far western end of an island, and headed toward a small dock where a single figure waited for us.

Benita waved and called, "Yoo-hoo, Ellison!" even though she must have known that the noise of the motors would keep her from being heard.

Ellison was bent and angular, with short-cropped, tight gray curls, and as we moved closer to the dock I could see the smooth, flat contours of his face, which was as dark and unwrinkled as a purple plum and just as empty of expression. Whatever he thought or felt seemed to be tucked safely out of sight behind the wire-rimmed glasses whose thick lenses shielded his eyes.

Beyond the dock and the heavily wooded hillside emerged the judge's large plantation house, which had obviously been designed to overlook the bay and its inviting strip of white sand. Maybe I had expected too much from Benita's enthusiastic description. The house had a grayed, slightly moldy look, and unkempt vines wrapped clinging tendrils over porch rails, pillars, and shutters.

With a softly padded thump the boat slid against the dock. The deckhands again sprang into view and into action, and, one by one, we were helped from the boat.

For the most part we took care of our own luggage, since we'd brought very little, but Ellison carried the judge's case up the path and entered the house, Kurt right behind him.

The others made trivial chatter about the boat trip and the house, but I hung back, absorbing the silent beauty of the island. The water, which patted the shore with little shushing sounds, was so clear that it was hard to judge its depth. Under its shimmering surface was a display of purple and red sea urchins and strange, small plants with wiggling fingerlike leaves. A few tiny golden fish, who looked like frantic escapees from an aquarium, darted together through the leaves, whirled, and shot out to deeper water. I could hardly wait to get into my bathing suit.

Suddenly self-conscious, I said, "I'm coming," to no one at all, and looked up toward Madelyn, whom I knew must be the one I felt staring at me.

But Madelyn was in animated conversation with Norton, and the others were just as intent on their stroll to the steps to the veranda. I studied the house. Someone was watching me. I could feel it. A guest? Another servant?

There were no faces at any of the windows, but the feeling of being watched was so strong that I turned in a semicircle, my eyes trying to pierce the tangle of trees and shrubs that crept almost down to the sea.

I saw no one. No one at all. So I picked up my bag and scrambled to catch up with the others.

Just as I joined them the boat motor started up again. We whirled to watch the boat backing away from the dock.

Norton took a few steps forward, as though he could stop the crew, and demanded, "Where are they taking the boat?"

"To Freeport," the judge said. He looked at Norton quizzically. "Does it matter?"

"Do you have other boats? Other transportation from this island?" He nervously cleared his throat a couple of times. "I—I don't like feeling—uh—closed in."

Benita's laughter rippled over us. "Closed in?" She raised her arms high. "With all this open beauty, how could you feel closed in?"

"Maybe I used the wrong word," he mumbled.

"If I said *trapped*, would you understand what I mean?"

"Claustrophobia takes a number of forms," Aldo said. "This concern that Norton feels could be called 'island fever.' "

Norton's head bobbed up and down in agreement. "That's it exactly." He peered up through his eyeshade at the judge. "When will the boat be back?"

"On Sunday afternoon," the judge said calmly. "When our business is concluded."

"Then let's get on with it."

Judge Arlington-Hughes held up both hands, palms out. "Slow down," he drawled, as though he were deliberately trying to be infuriating. "We have plenty of time. You've all given me your entire weekend."

"You know we're eager to see the topaz, Justin," Madelyn said. "Why don't you tell us when you'll show it to us?"

The judge smiled. He was obviously enjoying the mystery he'd created. "Directly to the point as always, Madelyn."

No one spoke. We all waited. With the boat gone a hush lay over the island. I could hear the whisper of the breeze through the trees and the occasional cry of a gull, even the slap of waves against the dock.

"Very well," he said. "If you'd like a schedule, you may have one. Ellison will direct you to your rooms. If there is anything you wish, you have only to ask. During the remainder of the afternoon you may entertain yourselves in any way you like.

There is swimming, and we can provide snorkeling equipment for those who are attuned to nature. There are trails through the woods, although I'd suggest that no one stray too far because, even though the island encompasses an area of only two square miles, it is possible to become lost. There are books to read in the library, and a few rocking chairs and reclining lawn chairs on the veranda for those who wish only to relax. Please be dressed for dinner by seven P.M. We'll have cocktails in the dining room at that time."

"Justin! Don't be so infuriating! What about the artifact?" Benita's lower lip curled out as she apparently tried for a cute pout. She missed.

"You'll see it tonight," the judge said. "A jewel as beautiful as the one I am going to display for you needs the proper setting."

"Oh, bother!" Benita snapped. "You're playing games with us."

Madelyn quickly said, "We asked for an itinerary, and Justin gave us one. Since the opportunity presents itself, I am going to take a leisurely nap."

"A nap?" Benita stared at Madelyn unbelievingly.

"A good idea," Aldo said. "I may follow it. The sea air has made me sleepy."

"I'll be in my room too," Norton grumbled. "As long as I have free time, I'll use it to go over some papers I brought along."

Benita looked from one face to another, then said, "Oh. Well, I may just read—in my room of course. If anyone wants me, that's where I'll be."

I wondered who they thought they were fooling. The judge better have a hideaway or he'd find them all descending upon him at once.

The judge turned to me. "Do you have plans, Andrea?"

It was the first time he had admitted that I existed. I was so surprised that I stammered, "I—I'm going swimming."

"Be very careful," he said. "There are no undercurrents to worry about, but there are plant-like sea animals that can sting and burn your feet painfully if you step on them."

"I know," I said. "I learned about them at our science museum."

"Maybe someone should go with you." Madelyn sounded a bit concerned.

No one spoke up. I hadn't expected anyone to. I said, "I'm a very good swimmer, and I plan to stay close to shore because I'm going to snorkel. You don't have to worry about me, Aunt Madelyn."

Ellison appeared in the open doorway. "Come along now with me," he said.

Like first-graders off on a field trip, we followed him across the entry hall and up the stairs in a neat and tidy line.

I was surprised that my room faced the ocean. Considering how the judge felt about me as an unwanted guest, I had halfway expected to be stuck in a closet. But after Ellison opened the shuttered doors that led to the veranda, spilling a shock of brightness over what had been dim outlines and shapes, I put down my bag and took a careful look at my surroundings. The walls had been painted a flat, glaring white, but there were smudges of mildew where they met the ceiling. And even though a breeze had begun to sift through the warm summer air, it couldn't completely dispel the musty, stale smell of a room that had been closed tightly for too long.

A white woven cotton spread and two plump pillows covered the bed, which had an ornate headboard of white-painted wrought iron. An old-fashioned chest of drawers stood at one side of the bed, a comfortable wicker chair with a blue cushion at the other. There were three doors in the room. One led to a small closet, one to the outside hall, and one to a narrow bathroom with a cramped shower stall just large enough to be called adequate if you didn't care how clean you got your elbows.

I stepped out on the second-story veranda and, from the corners of my eyes, saw someone pop quickly back into one of the rooms. Okay. I wasn't looking for company either. I closed the shutters and put on my bathing suit, quickly hanging up the few clothes I had brought with me.

With the shutters closed the room smelled even more musty, so I opened the outside doors wide. I wasn't worried about burglars or snoopers. I was probably the only one on this island with nothing worth stealing and nothing to hide.

Maybe all those nappers and resters had meant what they said. The house was suspiciously quiet as I went down the stairs two at a time to search out Ellison.

The rooms I looked into were dim, with ugly, out-of-date, overstuffed furniture. They would

never have made it into *Architectural Digest.*
Then it dawned on me that, since the judge owned
them, they were probably valuable antiques. On
one side of the entry hall was a smallish room with
lots of bookshelves stuffed with books across one
side. The air was so warm and damp that I could
actually smell the mustiness that infected the
books. Beyond this library was a large office with
windows on two sides, but the shutters over the
windows were closed. Obviously I wasn't going to
find Ellison around here.

I strolled back the way I had come, poking my
head into what seemed to be a living room on the
opposite side of the entry hall. It wasn't an inviting
place. There were groupings of sofas, mismatched
tables of all sizes, and clustered chairs. There was a
wide louvered door at the far end, but the louvers
had been pushed to each side, showing a large
dining room.

A soft voice behind me made me jump at least
three inches into the air. "Is there something you
were looking for, miss?"

"Ellison!" I said, staggering into a quick turn and
leaning against the doorframe. "I was looking for
you. The judge said something about some snorkel
stuff. Do you know where I can find it?"

He nodded solemnly. "We'll get you a mask, a
tube, and flippers. Come with me now."

"Sure," I said, and trotted to keep up with him.
"Have you worked here long?"

"Yes, miss," he said.

"How many people work here?"

"I work here. That's enough."

"Oh," I said. "I thought maybe the judge had a cook."

"I do the cooking."

"Oh." It was very hard to think of anything else to say, so I gave up.

Ellison opened a cupboard, rummaged through it, and brought out some really neat equipment. I tried on some fins that turned out to be too big, but Ellison was able to tuck them back on the shelf and come up with a pair just the right size.

"There're many, many poisonous plant animals in the sea," he said. His eyes, behind those thick lenses, shimmered as though they were underwater.

"Yes. I know about them. I'll watch out," I said.

"Use the ladder at the end of the dock when you go in the water."

"Okay, I will."

"Don't swim too far," he told me.

"I won't." I put the mask on the back of my head, scooped up the fins and tube, and hurried out of the house and down to the beach, eager to get away from Ellison—from all of them.

The sand slipped between my toes like warm silk. I stooped to pick up a small, curved shell, then threw it away. Lots of time left for shell hunting. Maybe I'd even be able to dive for the big pink-pearl-lined conch. The wooden deck burned the soles of my feet, so I ran to the end and climbed on the ladder, slipping on the fins and dropping into the surprisingly warm water. I swished the mask through the water and put it on, making sure it was snug. Then out I swam over a scene of flashing, weaving color so intricate and lovely, I could hardly bear not to share it with someone else.

I wished I could share it with Rick.

It hurt to know that I couldn't. My throat was so tight, it was hard to swallow. I ached so hard for Rick that I wondered if he could somehow sense it. I wanted to pretend that he was beside me, that soon he'd reach out, touching my arm, pointing at a bright-blue fish he wanted me to see.

"Grow up, Andy," he had said.

Maybe Rick was right. Maybe I was too dramatic and stubborn about causes. I could change. I could try to be the way he wanted me to be.

Tears suddenly blinded me. I shook my head, almost choking on a mouthful of salt water. Tearing off my mask, gasping and choking, I finally managed to breathe normally again. That's what I got for not paying attention to what I was doing.

I treaded water, glancing around me. The house and beach were nowhere in sight. I had somehow entered a small cove where palms, broad-leafed shrubs, and some kind of red-flowering trees crowded right down to the edge of the water. Below me, through the crystal water, was an equally brilliant garden, dotted with the large, curved shells of the conch. A promontory of bare limestone rock jutted out into the sea ahead of me. Water had worn large holes in the rock, and I could see through one of them to another cove beyond.

Curious, I swam ahead, my fins giving me an extra speed, and discovered that the rock arched just under the waterline. Below the arch was an entrance to the other cove, and to the left of the cove was an opening—only partly covered with water—to a cave.

I had to see the cave. There was no way I could pass up a cave. Pulling my mask into place and taking an extra-deep breath, I dived under the arch, made a right turn, and swam into a cavern so dark and still, I knew I had made a mistake. I had no right to be there.

CHAPTER

~~~~~~~~~~~~~~~

5

The ceiling to the cave was high, rough, and deeply curved, the walls about fifteen feet apart. It was like the inside of a bubble, with only its entrance to break the roundness and let in light. It was dark toward the back of the cave, so I couldn't tell how deep it might be. My first thought was to wonder if something might be hiding in the dark water. An octopus? Large, scuttling crabs? But I wasn't afraid. Anything that lived in this cave would be as withdrawn and secret as the cave itself. A ledge lay to my left, so I hoisted myself up, careful not to scratch myself on the rough stone and the clusters of barnacles that were plastered to it. I rested there for a moment between two small tidal pools and gently poked the end of my snorkel tube into the center of a flowering sea anemone, which quickly closed its spidery arms around the tube.

Discoloration on the walls of the cave, damp though they were, showed me how high the sea would rise. It came up only a few feet; there were bleached and dried ledges and nooks and hollows in the porous limestone walls far above the water-line.

What a good hiding place, I thought, and my mind flicked at the possibilities of a lovely adventure with pirates and plunder before I smiled to myself, put my mask back on, and swam out of the cave.

I twisted to swim through the arch and propelled myself—a little faster now—in the direction of the judge's dock. The sun was much lower, casting a deep orange glow that glimmered on the surface of the water. A dark shadow slipped past me as I neared the dock, and I picked up my pace, recognizing the thin, mean lines of a barracuda and eager to stay out of its way.

Once on the ladder I could pull off the fins and scramble up to the surface of the dock. I tugged off my mask and shook water from my hair as though I were a pup. Smoothing it back from my forehead, enjoying the feel of the sun on my wet body, I was once again aware of being watched. The prying eyes irritated me, but I wouldn't let the watcher know it. Slowly I walked across the dock and up the path toward the house.

Aunt Madelyn, dressed in dark blue silk, which set off her long strand of pearls, stepped out on the lower veranda and called, "Andrea! You haven't allowed yourself much time to dress for dinner!" As I climbed the steps to join her she murmured with concern, "Dinner will be served in less than

half an hour. Are you going to be able to do anything with that dripping wet hair?"

"Don't worry." I shook my hair again. "I
wouldn't go anywhere without my trusty hair
dryer."

I expected her to relax, but she looked even
more concerned and said, "Let's hope the generator can handle it."

"Generator?" It suddenly occurred to me that
the island wouldn't be magically supplied with
electricity. The judge would have to manufacture
his own. "I'll hurry," I told her, and I did, banging
my elbows only twice while I showered. I dressed
in a red, loose-knit cotton sweater and full poplin
skirt in matching red, which I liked because between the two pieces there were six deep pockets.
I found a stick of gum in one pocket and two quar-
ters in another, which was a nice surprise. Brush in
hand, I plugged in my hair dryer. It started, then
just as suddenly it stopped.

There were quick footsteps on the stairs and
down the hallway. "Andrea!" Madelyn called from
outside my door. "You've blown out the generator.
Don't use your hair dryer again!"

I opened the door. "I'm sorry." My stomach
rumbled, and I realized how hungry I was. "I
ruined dinner, didn't I?"

"No. The stove is fueled with butane gas," she
said. "But dinner will be served promptly at
seven, and you have only five minutes left. You
must not be late!"

"What about the generator?"

She sighed elaborately. "No doubt we'll eat by

candlelight. Ellison will probably work on the generator between courses."

"I'm sorry."

"Don't waste time making apologies. Hurry!"

"I'll hurry!" I said. "I'll be downstairs on time!"

And I was, my still-damp hair slicked back and twisted into a tight knot at the back of my neck. The one, lone barrette that I found in the bottom of a third pocket had the great responsibility of holding the knot in place. I hoped it would stay put, at least until after dessert.

I jogged down the stairs, across the wide entry hall, and into the living room. The appearance of the room had been changed, not all of it due to a cluster of lit candles on a table near the dining-room entrance. There was a more interesting table—a narrow, high table with spindly legs, which I had seen earlier beside one of the sofas. It was performing a special duty of its own. It had been moved to one side of the room and draped with a black velvet cloth. Behind the table was a chair, equally ugly and probably equally valuable as an antique. Next to the table stood a modern spot-light type of floor lamp, its spot aimed at the middle of the table. The cone-shaped shade and stand were covered with a silvery chrome, dingy and scraped in places. It seemed completely out of place.

The judge wasn't in the room. Neither was Kurt. Madelyn and Norton had their heads together, and Benita stood aside with Aldo, the two of them studying the setting with silent suspicion.

Ellison appeared at the entrance to the dining

room and formally apologized because dinner
would be delayed half an hour. Then he announced that drinks would be served on the veranda.

The judge presided, but not very graciously. He
was downright grumpy and glared at me, once
mumbling, "Persona non grata." I didn't have to
ask for a translation. I quickly glanced around, my
face hot with embarrassment, desperately hoping
that no one else had heard him. It was horrible to
be an unwanted guest.

As Madelyn and Benita gave their orders I decided that everyone would be more comfortable if
I weren't in sight, so I stepped back through the
open terrace doors into the living room. As I did
someone slipped from the room and disappeared
into the entry hall. It was just a flash of movement.
I didn't see who it was. It would have to be Ellison.
Everyone else was out on the veranda. Right?

But I heard a sound from the opposite direction
—the dining room—and turned to see Ellison put-
tering with something on the dining-room table.

Curious, I stepped to the open veranda doors
and began to count noses. Madelyn was talking to
the judge. Benita sat in a nearby wicker rocker,
sipping on her drink. At the far end of the veranda, opposite the library, Norton leaned against
the porch rail and seemed to be staring through
the darkness, studying what little could be seen of
the sea.

The person who had left the room in such a
hurry must have been Aldo. I shrugged. I could
practically hear Mom telling me not to be dra-

matic. As though to emphasize her point, I could hear footsteps down the stairs and across the entry hall. I leaned in to see Aldo striding across the living room toward me. He smiled and said something about being glad he'd had time to go back to his room. He'd realized he was missing a cuff link, and there it had been—lying on the bed. I was glad he didn't know how suspicious I'd been, and for no good reason. That strange, black-covered table had ignited my imagination.

Aldo stepped onto the veranda, and I followed. Norton, Benita, and Madelyn were clustered around the judge.

Aunt Madelyn put a hand on my shoulder and drew me into the group. "Did you have a lovely swim, Andrea?" she asked.

"Yes," I said. "The sea flowers are beautiful."

The judge looked up. "Some of those beautiful 'flowers' can be deadly. Things are not always what they seem."

I thought about Rick and sighed. "People, too," I said.

The judge gave such an odd laugh that everyone looked at him. "An astute remark, my dear," he said. "Especially in this group."

I was puzzled. Was he making fun of me? "I don't understand," I told him. "Do you mean that someone here isn't for real?"

"There's an old nautical term," he said. " 'Sailing under false colors.' "

I could feel Madelyn tense. No one responded. I got the feeling that the judge didn't expect anyone to.

To my relief, Ellison appeared just then and announced dinner.

"Please go ahead without me," Aldo said. "I'll join you in a few minutes."

"What's the problem?" the judge asked.

"A slight sinus headache," Aldo said. "I have some aspirin in my room. Please. I insist. Don't wait for me."

"Very well," the judge said. We followed him into the dining room.

The meal, which *was* served by candlelight, was boring. Ellison wasn't the greatest cook in the world. It was hard to see everything I was eating, which was probably for the best. I sat at the end of the table next to Kurt, who, when he wasn't substituting for Ellison in bringing more rolls or water, tried to relate to me by reminiscing about his high school football career.

"I bet you dated the head cheerleader too," I said.

His expression became a little wistful, and he held his knife and fork at rest for a few moments. "I was really somebody in high school," he said. "Everybody wanted to be my friend. I never had to worry about a girl turning me down when I asked for a date, and yeah, I did date the head cheerleader. We even fell in love—for a while."

I didn't know what to say to that, so I just looked at him and hoped I'd think of something. But he shoveled a large bite of steak into his mouth and said around it, "It was never the same after high school."

"Maybe you should have gone out for pro ball," I suggested.

He sighed. "Maybe I should have, but it's too late now." Deliberately, he seemed to be changing the subject away from himself. "What do you want to be when you grow up?"

I got the same warm feeling inside that I always got when I thought about Dr. Kirschman. "I think I want to be an archaeologist," I said.

Kurt gave me a quick sideways glance, then shrugged.

There was no point in talking to Kurt about archaeology. Besides, I wanted to know more about him. "What do you do as the judge's secretary?" I asked. "Do you type letters and answer phones and all that?"

He shook his head. "I'm just one of his secretaries. He has office help who work with the phone and mail and all the other jobs office secretaries do. I handle other things for him."

He stopped there, so I asked, "Like what?"

"All sorts of things, like making sure the boat is ready when he wants to take it out. It's too complicated to go into right now."

I felt sorry for this guy, whose biggest moments in life had to have been back in high school. It hadn't taken me long to realize that the judge must be a pain to work for.

Kurt shoved back his chair and picked up my plate. "I'll help," I said.

He shook his head. "Sit down. You're a guest, and I'm paid to do this sort of thing."

So while he cleared the table and brought on

dessert, I joined the others in listening to the judge, who, naturally, sat at the head of the table and pontificated. He began some long-winded, uninteresting story about the IRS and a major art purchase, so I tuned him out. I thought about Mom and Dad and desperately hoped they were getting their problems worked out. I was homesick for a home that might not be there when I got back to Texas, and the thought was so scary I had to fight away the tears.

Suddenly Benita began to choke, waving her hands in the air and jumping from her chair.

"Pound her on the back!" Norton jumped up too.

But Benita managed to recover enough to say, "No. I'm all right." She coughed again and said, "Water. It went down the wrong way." She tried to smother another coughing fit as she hurried from the room.

The judge began to question Aldo about his travels, but Madelyn suddenly said, "I'd better make sure that Benita's all right." She pushed back her chair and left the room.

Aldo began to describe the details of some restaurant he liked in Monaco, and even though we had just eaten, his descriptions of the meals made me hungry.

About the time that I began to wonder what was taking Aunt Madelyn so long, she returned and slid back into her chair without a word. At the same time the overhead lights came on. We all blinked and squinted at each other in the sudden light.

Ellison appeared in the kitchen doorway and solemnly said, "The generator got fixed."

"Obviously," the judge answered.

Kurt had served us some kind of soppy pudding for dessert. Now that we could see it, no one seemed to want to eat it, which was just as well, because the judge stood up, tapping on his water glass. However, instead of giving an after-dinner speech, he said, "As soon as Benita returns, we'll be ready to begin."

Benita, still a little out of breath, spoke from the doorway to the living room. "Ooooh, such tantalizing mystery! Are we to have a treasure hunt?"

Judge Arlington-Hughes scowled at her. "Hunt, no. Treasure, yes. You are invited to come to the parlor to view the Peruvian artifact."

It was like the bell announcing the end of class on the last day of school. Everyone frantically shoved back chairs, fumbling and scrambling as they tried not to trip over or step on the others in the general movement toward the living room.

I hung back, feeling more like an outsider than ever. I wasn't really part of this group. But Kurt stepped up behind me and held my shoulders, giving me a gentle push forward. "Go ahead," he said. "There's a candle for you."

"A candle?"

"On the table."

"Look," I said, turning toward him and lowering my voice, "I feel a little bit guilty about joining them. The judge didn't want me to come. I can't bid on that artifact."

"You want to see it, don't you?"

"Yes, but maybe later. Right now this is some kind of a big moment for him."

"For you, too, unless you stay here talking and miss it," he answered, and pulled the louvered doors closed between us.

Curiosity was stronger than guilt, so I willingly turned and stepped into the living room. The only light in the room came from the candles that Aunt Madelyn, Benita, Norton, and Aldo were holding and the solitary candle in a small brass candle holder on a nearby marble-topped table. I picked it up and joined the others, who were standing in a semicircle in front of the velvet-draped table, squeezing in between Aunt Madelyn and Benita. The flickering light distorted their features and cast giant, jerking shadows on the wall. The four adults were gripping their candles, not moving, not breathing, just staring at Judge Arlington-Hughes. I discovered that I was doing the same thing.

The judge hadn't waited for me before beginning his show. From the few words I heard as I joined the group, he had been delivering some kind of short history of the artifact. He pulled a dark box from his coat pocket and paused, smiling.

"I want you to get your first glimpse of the stone under the spell of candlelight."

He opened the box and laid the artifact on the black velvet in front of us, then leaned back in his chair.

We all gasped. I had never seen anything like that in my life, not even in some of the photographs that Dr. Sammy Kirschman had shown us.

The topaz, which had to be even larger across than a silver dollar, was roughly cut, not faceted. But it was as deeply blue as seawater and sparkled with a gold sheen, the way the ocean had sparkled in the late afternoon sunlight.

The stone was ringed in gold, that ancient, deep yellow gold, soft and unevenly thick on three sides. I first thought that the top of the gold frame was lumpy and uneven with an awkward loop, but as I studied it the lumps became the figure and curling tail of a pinched-faced monkey—an insanely grinning monkey with tiny sharp paws that clutched the top of the topaz. I was drawn to the stone, yet at the same time that horrible monkey made me shiver.

The judge ordered, "Blow out your candles. Now we'll see the artifact in its full glory under the spotlight."

The others did, but I hesitated. I wanted to wait until the light came on. I didn't want to be in this creepy house in the dark. It's just as well that I didn't follow orders.

Looking smug while the others were puffing out their candle flames, the judge turned the switch on the lamp, but nothing happened. He wiggled the bulb in the cone of the lamp, then glanced down at the floor.

"Drat!" he exploded. "That stupid Kurt! This lamp was supposed to be plugged in!"

The others were now concerned with what the judge was doing. I forgot that I didn't belong here. I had even forgotten my manners. How often while I was growing up had I heard "Look, don't touch!" And yet with nothing but the artifact on my mind, while everyone's attention was diverted, I reached out to touch that stone.

It slid under my fingertips as smoothly as tidal-pool water, scummy and warm from the summer sun. For just an instant it lay under my hand.

I don't know exactly what happened next, because it all took place too quickly. I was aware that the judge had bent down to plug in the lamp, but at the same time everyone seemed to move forward. I was jostled aside. The candle was knocked from my hand and went out. In the darkness there was a cry and a crackling, sizzling sound, a thump and a crash.

Terrified, not knowing what was taking place, I dropped to the floor, trying to roll into a ball. I heard someone scream, but it wasn't me. I was making little whimpering noises to myself, wishing I were home, desperately wanting to be off this horrible island and back with my parents.

I heard running footsteps, and what sounded like people bumping and slamming into things. Voices were shouting "Where are the matches?" "Light the candles!" "What happened?" Then Aunt Madelyn, practically next to my ear, screamed, "Andrea!"

I opened my eyes and looked directly into the wide-open, sightless eyes of Judge Arlington-Hughes, whose bloodless face was just inches away from mine.

CHAPTER

~~~~~~~~~~~~~~~~

6

Without consciously thinking about what I was doing, I scuttled backward as fast as I could go. I know that I connected with someone's leg and for an instant got tangled in the black velvet cloth that lay on the floor next to the overturned table. "He's dead, he's dead, he's dead!" I was screeching.

Strong hands grabbed me and jerked me to my feet. "Stop that," Aldo demanded, so I did.

It was hard to breathe, and my legs had about as much strength as our dinner pudding, so I stumbled into the nearest chair.

Kurt, who had been bending over the judge, got to his feet. He stared down at the judge as though he were trying to figure out what had happened.

"Well?" Norton demanded.

Kurt slowly turned to look at him. "He's dead," he said.

"What was it?" Benita whimpered. "Did Justin have a heart attack?"

"Nothing wrong with the judge's heart," Ellison said. "The man been younger and fitter than me."

"But he was just sitting there," Benita said.

"No," Madelyn said. "Remember? He was fiddling with the lamp. It wouldn't turn on, and he complained that Kurt was supposed to plug it in and hadn't."

"I'm sure I plugged it in," Kurt said.

Norton shook his head. "No, no. I was at that end of the table. I could see Justin reach down, pick up the plug, and put it into the wall socket."

"Then everything went dark," Benita added. She was so pale that I hoped she'd decide to sit down, too, before she fell down. I shivered and tried to squirm more deeply into the puffy upholstery.

Kurt frowned. "I don't understand what happened. The judge told me what he planned to do. You were all supposed to see the topaz by candlelight. Then he'd tell you to blow out your candles, and in the next instant he'd turn on the lamp." He turned to Norton. "But you just said that you saw him plug in the lamp. How could you see this?"

I spoke up. "I was afraid of the dark so I waited to blow out my candle."

"But Benita said it went dark when the judge plugged in the lamp."

"Somebody shoved me, and I dropped the candle holder, and the candle went out."

"Who shoved you?"

"I don't know. Everybody seemed to push forward at the same time."

Benita shuddered and in a small voice said, "Someone pushed me too."

The lamp was lying on its side. Aldo stooped to pick it up. His fingers slid along the cord, and he held up the plug end for us to see. The wrapping around the cord had been sliced and peeled back. "Judge Arlington-Hughes was upset that the lamp hadn't been plugged in," Aldo said. "Apparently he didn't see the state of this cord. When he plugged in the lamp his fingers must have connected with the bare wire." He dropped the cord. "It looks as though he was electrocuted."

"It's the fault of that awful lamp! Where did it come from?" Madelyn demanded.

"It belong to me," Ellison said. "The judge say he wants a spotlight, and that was the only lamp around here could do it. I got it out of the store-room. Nobody been using it for a long time, but I didn't see nothing wrong with the cord. Somebody maybe could have done that to the cord. On purpose."

Kurt frowned as he thought. "I'm sure there was nothing wrong with that cord when I put the lamp there."

"Did you plug in the lamp?" Aldo asked.

"I thought I had. I was supposed to. But the judge was wanting me to do one thing after another, and I may have forgotten."

"The assumption that the cord was stripped is ridiculous," Madelyn said. "That would mean that someone deliberately . . ." She didn't finish the sentence.

Norton stared at Kurt. "Someone who knew what the judge's plan was to be."

Kurt took a step backward. "I didn't kill the judge! Sure, I knew about his plan in advance. So did Ellison. But the rest of you could figure it out as soon as you saw the table all draped up with that black velvet and the lamp next to it. It could have been anyone here in this room!"

Every now and then the candles flickered. Each time they did our shadows leapt and jumped as though they were involved in a crazy kind of dance. I wrapped my arms around my shoulders, hugging myself, fighting against the cold that shivered like streaks of lightning up and down my back.

"This makes no sense," Madelyn said. "Why should someone kill Justin?"

"For the artifact," Benita said.

"But we were going to bid for it."

Benita shrugged. "Maybe someone didn't want to take the chance of losing it."

"But who would want it enough to murder for it?"

"You ought to know the answer to that," Benita said slowly. "Getting possession of it for the Sartington meant a great deal to you, didn't it, Madelyn?"

I gasped, remembering another acquisition Madelyn had mentioned not long ago. But "I would have killed to get it" had to be a figure of speech. Surely Madelyn wouldn't really murder anyone.

Madelyn could have won a prize in a haughtiness contest. Coolly she said, "You're being absurd, as usual, Benita. If you attempt to think logically—if that's possible—you'll realize that I'm the one person who would not have murdered to get possession of the stone. The Sartington collection is open to the public. Ergo, the artifact appears, and it's obvious that I had taken it."

She shook her head, and her eyes bored into those of her three competitors by turn. "Benita represents an art auction house and goodness knows who else, since it's possible that she could be involved in some secret dealing. She's done it before."

"Well, really!" Benita exploded. "There's nothing wrong in—"

But Aunt Madelyn hadn't finished. Imperiously, she held up a hand and continued. "Norton, of course, is here for his elusive employer, Franklin Granakee, in whose private collection the stone would be just as elusive. And off in some Mideastern country the person Aldo represents could possess the artifact in secret forever."

The three angrily denied the accusations until Kurt suddenly raised his voice. He was holding the black velvet cloth and the empty jewel case. "Where is the artifact?"

It was easy to see that it was not on the floor.

Benita gingerly pointed at the judge's body. "Why—uh—Justin must have it."

Kurt shook his head. "It wasn't in his hands or under his body. I checked."

All of them moved aimlessly, searching the floor

and the tables, as if they could see the artifact in plain sight if they just stared hard enough.

I got up and walked over to Aunt Madelyn. I was so frightened that I needed to be close to someone.

"No point in looking around," Kurt said. "And no point in looking anyplace else. Nobody had time to get out of this room, put that thing somewhere, and get back in again before the candles got lit."

"He could have hidden it in a vase or drawer or someplace like that," Benita suggested, which set off a rapid, fumbling search.

I pressed back out of the way, against the wall, wondering why one of the antiques didn't get broken.

They came up empty-handed, all of them migrating to the center of the room.

"Obviously, the murderer has the topaz," Benita said.

"Then the next step is obvious," Madelyn said. "A personal search."

"Absolutely not," Norton said.

"Oh?" Madelyn's dark eyebrows rose dramatically. "You must have a strong reason for refusing."

"I do," he snapped. He was so hyper that if he had jumped into the air, I wouldn't have been surprised. "To begin with, a personal search would be a great indignity. But the most important reason is that none of us can trust any of the others. Would you want to be searched by Justin's murderer?"

"I wouldn't," Kurt said quickly.

"I wouldn't either!" Benita cried.

Madelyn shrugged. "I agree."

I studied each in turn, wondering if one of them had killed Judge Arlington-Hughes. I forced myself to take a deep breath and think logically. "Dr. Kirschman always pointed out that we had to study scientific evidence before reaching a conclusion," I said. "We can't just decide by ourselves that the judge was murdered. Maybe it was only an accident." I didn't believe what I'd just told them, and it was obvious from their expressions that they didn't believe me either.

Aunt Madelyn's lips were tight. "Andrea, be realistic."

"I'm just trying to say that it's up to the police to make the decision."

Norton's voice was high and tight, and I could see him clenching and unclenching his fingers. "Of course we must call the police. There are things they should know. We can't stay trapped here on this island with—with a dead body."

"There's no telephone," Kurt told him. "The judge liked to really get away from it all."

"Ham radio, then?"

"The only broadcast radio was on the boat."

"What about on the rest of this island?" Benita asked, her fingers plucking nervously at the fringe on a small pillow. "Are there other people living here? Anyone who could help?"

"No. It's just undeveloped property. The island belonged to the judge, and his is the only house on it."

"Surely there must be some way we can reach

the authorities," Aldo demanded. He paused. "What country governs this island?"

"The Bahama Islands government," Kurt said. "The nearest office is in Freeport."

"How do we get there?"

"Only by boat, and the judge's boat won't be back until Sunday afternoon."

"Maybe we could send up a signal," Madelyn suggested. "Like a bonfire. Yes! Maybe we could light a large bonfire down on the beach. Would that bring a passing boat?"

"I doubt it," Kurt said. *"If* a boat happened to be passing, which isn't too likely, anyone on it would just think we were having a beach party and would leave us alone."

"What about the other islands in the Bahama Banks?" I asked. "We saw some houses and boats when we came in here. Could we reach any of those islands?"

"You probably didn't realize how far apart the inhabited islands were," Kurt said. "It would be a good long swim, if anyone could even make it."

I shivered. "With sharks and barracuda."

Madelyn pushed open all the doors to the veranda, as though in some way that would help. It was dark outside, with little moonlight. "We must think in an orderly fashion," she said. "It's our only help." She whirled to look at Ellison. "How soon can you repair the generator?"

Ellison's glasses mirrored the candlelight so that I couldn't see his eyes. "No way I can start work on it till morning," he said.

Madelyn gave him one of her looks. "How did you fix it earlier? It was dark then."

"Not at first. I got a good start before dark, so I knew what I was doing. Then I use the lantern and finish up."

"Lantern?" Benita perked up. "You mean you've got some other sources of light beyond these pitiful candles?"

"Yes, Miz Robley," Ellison said. "We got a couple of lanterns and some flashlights. Soon as we take care of everything, I get them for you."

"Thank goodness!" Benita dropped onto the nearest sofa and laid a hand over her heart. "This has been exhausting! I am absolutely longing to get to bed!"

"While Justin is left lying here on the floor?" Madelyn asked. Benita gave a little shriek, and Madelyn turned to Ellison. "You know this place the best. What can we do with his body?"

"There's a walk-in freezer," Ellison said. "We can use that."

"That sounds like a sensible idea," Aldo said, but I interrupted.

"When a crime is committed, aren't you supposed to leave everything the way it was until the police come so they can look for clues?"

"In a case like this, no," Kurt said. "It's more important to take care of the body."

"Besides," Madelyn said, "what clues could there be, except for the lamp? Each of us had access to the room and to the lamp, and when the crime happened we were all present."

"No, we weren't," I said. "Kurt and Ellison weren't here. They were in the kitchen."

They looked at each other. "Maybe so," Ellison said. "I think Mr. Cameron may be in the kitchen, but I wasn't there. I was in the bathroom."

Benita put her hands against her ears and squeezed her eyelids tightly shut. "Stop it! Stop it! I can't stand all this!" she cried. "Everybody's accusing everyone else, and we don't know who the murderer is!"

"*If* there was a murder," I mumbled.

She ignored me, wailed, "I'm frightened!" and began to cry.

Norton pulled a handkerchief from his pocket, shoved it into one of her hands, then stood by and looked uncomfortable.

"Come on," Kurt said to the others as he bent to tug over the small area rug, "lend me a hand. If we roll the body onto this, we can carry it or drag it into the freezer."

"Wait a minute," I told them. "At least let me take some pictures of—of the judge with my camera."

"There's not enough light," Aldo said.

"Ellison could bring in the lanterns," Benita suggested.

"It doesn't matter," I said. "The camera has a good flash, and it's loaded with superfast film. I can get some clear pictures."

"It's a waste of time," Norton grumbled. He stepped forward and said to Kurt, "Let's get this job over with."

"No!" Madelyn took command. "We'll want the

police to know that we tried to cooperate in every way possible. I think Andrea's suggestion is a good one. Please wait, and I'll get the camera from my room." She picked up a candle and went upstairs with such authority that no one moved.

Benita sniffled a few more times, ruining Norton's handkerchief with her runny mascara. Norton walked to the open veranda doors and stood there, hands shoved into his pockets, probably hoping that if he looked hard enough, he could see help coming. Aldo stood silently, as closed in as a cupboard with locked doors. Ellison sat on the nearest chair, hands clasped between his knees, and Kurt stepped back, so that his features weren't in the direct light, but I could see him carefully and slowly studying the others.

Aunt Madelyn returned quickly with the camera, and I took six or seven pictures of the judge's body, aiming from different directions. Once I pointed the camera upward and Norton snapped, "Stick to the subject. You don't need snapshots of the rest of us."

It was a horrible job. I hated to look. I began to feel sick to my stomach.

Finally Aldo took my shoulders and steered me away from the body, "That's enough," he said. He motioned to Kurt to join him and he bent over, clasping the judge under his arms. Ellison came to help. Reluctantly, Norton edged toward them, waited until they had positioned the judge's body on the rug, and gingerly took hold of one of the four corners.

"Through the dining room and the kitchen,"

Kurt said. "The door to the walk-in freezer is at the far end of the kitchen."

With a great deal of grunting and puffing, they managed to hoist the makeshift litter and stagger with it out of the room.

Benita blew her nose and glanced around to make sure no one besides the three of us was in earshot. "Madelyn!" she hissed. "I'm terrified! I want to sleep in your room!"

"You can't," Madelyn said. "My room has only one twin bed."

"I don't care! I'll sleep on the floor!"

"Benita, dear, I greatly value my privacy. You can sleep in your own room and in your bed."

"But the murderer—"

"We're not sure that Justin was murdered. And if he was, whoever murdered him is not going to murder you."

"Don't be so sure of yourself, Madelyn. You have no way of knowing that!"

"Think about it. Be logical. Suppose that Justin *was* murdered. During the confusion the artifact disappeared. Therefore, the murderer has what he was after."

"Oh." Benita sank back against the cushions on the sofa.

"Not necessarily," I said.

They both turned to stare at me, and I added, "Well, you're guessing, aren't you? You can't be sure where the artifact is, because it didn't show up. Maybe the murderer has the artifact, maybe not."

Benita made a funny noise in the back of her

throat, and Aunt Madelyn snapped, "Oh, honestly, Andrea! Just when I had her calmed down!"

"In spite of what happened, I see no reason for any of us to fear the others." Aldo spoke from the doorway to the dining room, and I could see Norton and Kurt standing beside him.

"Oh no?" Norton sneered. "There's a good possibility that a murderer is in our midst, we're trapped on this island, and you see no reason for any of us to be afraid?"

"I agree with Norton," Madelyn said quickly, sneaking a quick look at Benita. "The only possible reason for murder was to obtain the artifact. That seems to have been accomplished."

Kurt stepped forward. "I'm sorry, Benita, that this happened and that you're so frightened. Since I worked for the judge I feel responsible for doing whatever I can to help. In the morning I'll try to swim to the nearest inhabited island."

"You can't!" I exclaimed.

Madelyn scowled. "I thought you said it was too far away. Are you a good swimmer?"

Kurt shrugged. "Fair. I can hold my own in the water. That's about it."

She looked at me. "Didn't you say there are sharks in the water?"

"Yes," I said, "and barracuda too."

"Then we'll rule that out as totally impractical," Madelyn told him. "It would be stupid for you to take such a desperate chance and probably lose your life." Maybe she realized how harsh she sounded, because her voice softened a bit and she added, "Although the offer was a gracious gesture on your part."

Norton glared at her. I knew he wouldn't care who did what as long as he got off this island.

"Look out ahead," Ellison called, and as the men in the doorway parted he came in laden with the lanterns and flashlights he had promised. Each of them took what was wanted, which left me with candlelight.

"Sorry," Kurt said. He held up his candlestick to show that we were both at the bottom of the list. "There weren't enough to go around."

"Candles are fine if I can have a spare," I said.

I hung my camera strap around my neck, picked up one of the lit candles in its holder, two others, and a book of matches and walked toward the stairs, carefully shielding my candle flame, which jumped so wildly that it threatened to go out. "See you in the morning," I said to the others.

"Where are you going?" Madelyn asked me.

"To bed," I said. "I don't think there's anything else left to do, is there?"

"Why, no, I guess not," she answered.

Benita scurried to catch up with me. She held her lantern carefully out in front of her, where its beam of light slammed into shadows and sent them sprawling. "Wait for me. I'll go up with you."

"I will too," Madelyn suddenly decided, and joined us on the stairs.

At the door to Benita's room we practically had to peel her off and show her how to lock her door.

Then we came to mine.

"Are you sure you'll be all right?" Madelyn

asked me, and I could see the real concern in her eyes.

"As all right as it's possible to be."

"You can sleep in my room if you want to."

I knew that was offering a lot. Madelyn was right when she said she valued her privacy. I touched her arm. "Thanks," I said. "I appreciate the offer, but my door has a good lock on it too."

"Be sure you keep the veranda doors tightly locked also."

I nodded, but I had no intention of doing so. Without the breeze from the sea the room would be suffocatingly hot.

Madelyn rested a hand on my arm. "Perhaps I should have paid attention to your hunch," she said. "I'm sorry that I brought you into this."

"You couldn't have known what would happen," I told her.

She took a long breath. "I know I must seem harsh to you, but the Sartington—my position as curator—they mean everything to me. Maybe I should have left room in my life for other pursuits, but . . ." She stopped and shook her head. "My life is my work. There's no place in it for much more. Your mother—you—I do care for you. Oh, Andrea, I hope that you understand."

I still didn't feel comfortable with Aunt Madelyn, but I told her that I did understand. It seemed to be what she needed to hear, and at this moment I felt terribly sorry for her. "Good night, Aunt Madelyn," I added, and for the first time gave her a tentative kiss that landed somewhere in the air near her left ear.

"Thank you, Andrea," she said, looking pleased. "Good night."

I went into my room, still carefully shielding my candle flame, and firmly locked the door. The veranda doors were wide open to the night, as I had left them. I placed the candle holder, the extra candles, and the matches on the chest of drawers next to my bed and closed the veranda doors, locking them and making sure that the shutters were snugly shut.

Then I sat on the edge of the bed, close to the candlelight, reached into the deep, right-hand pocket of my skirt, and slowly pulled out the glimmering Peruvian artifact.

CHAPTER

~~~~~~~~~~

7

The topaz lay in my palm like a scooped-up handful of clear, turquoise seawater, glowing in the candlelight. But as the flame flickered the tiny monkey that gripped the stone seemed to move, and I could almost swear that he grinned as his eyes stared directly into mine. I kept my eyes away from him. He was primitive, roughly fashioned, and terrifying.

I couldn't believe that the artifact was in my possession. I hadn't intended it to be. Everything during that horrible moment in the living room had happened so quickly that I had reacted instinctively, clutching the stone and dropping to the floor as the darkness and sounds of death slammed into us. At some moment I realized that I was holding the stone and shoved it into my pocket. The artifact shouldn't be claimed by any of these greedy collectors, including my own Aunt Madelyn. It belonged to the people of Peru. Some-

how, I was going to see that it was returned to
them.

How? I wondered. Well, one thing at a time. I
wouldn't worry about that now. At the moment
there was only one thing to be concerned about.
The murderer wanted that artifact. If he had
killed for it, then sooner or later he was going to
come looking for it. I would have to find a good
place in which to hide it, but for the moment the
safest place was on my body.

I rummaged through my overnight case and
pulled out a narrow blue ribbon. I ran the ribbon
through the loop made by the monkey's tail and
tied the ends together. Then I slipped the ribbon
over my head and changed into my red-striped
cotton pajamas. I tucked the topaz underneath,
between my breasts, the sharp little monkey paws
scratching my skin. No one else would know that it
was there.

The room was getting awfully stuffy, and I
moved to the veranda doors. But I paused before
opening them. With my room wide open to the
night, I'd be vulnerable to anyone who came
prowling. Shivering, in spite of the heat, I rested
my head against their shutters. No one had suspected me. They seemed to be too busy suspecting
each other. My best defense was innocence. I
could open just a few of the shutters, but by opening my doors I would seem to have nothing to
hide.

With trembling fingers I unlatched the doors
and swung them wide. Clouds had covered the
moon, so the veranda was a dark, shadowless void

in which anyone could hide. I listened and thought I heard a footstep, a board that creaked under someone's weight.

Don't be dramatic, I told myself, as though I were Mom. Stumbling, shivering, I managed to make it into bed and blew out the candlelight. If only this were my own bed at home!

As my eyes became accustomed to the darkness I began to calm down. I could see outlines now of pillars and tree branches against a sky that was softer and less foreboding. Down on the beach wavelets made a rhythmic, comforting, shushing slap against the sand, and the breeze from the sea was cool. My eyes closed, I relaxed, and soon I was asleep.

I don't know how long I slept. I awoke hearing a squeaking sound that could have been part of the dream that fled from me while I tried to grab at its edges. Rick. The dream had been about Rick, but I was left with nothing but a lonely ache that also must have been part of the dream. The squeak came again. Confusion dissolved as I woke with a start, sucking in air and holding it, afraid even to breathe.

Someone was walking on the veranda, moving very slowly toward the open doors of my room.

There was nothing I could do but wait and watch. My eyelids were glued upward, my steady gaze on the open doorway.

Another creak of boards, and a white figure appeared, silhouetted against the night. Before I could move it swooped toward me. I opened my mouth to scream, but all that came out was a kind of deep, scratchy gasp.

"Andrea!" the white figure whispered. "It's just me! Benita!"

I scrambled to a sitting position, and she perched on the edge of my bed. "Your doors were open. How in the world could you sleep with your doors open? Did you know they were open? Well, of course you did."

"What's the matter?" I managed to whisper back. "Why did you wake me up?"

"I'm sorry I woke you," she murmured. "Well, I'm not really, because I had to wake someone, and your doors were the only ones open. Weren't you afraid to leave them open?"

"Why did you have to wake someone?" I wanted to get her back on the track. I was catching her jitters, and I didn't want them.

"Because of the noise in the room on the far side of mine. Norton's room."

"What kind of a noise?"

She thought a moment, then whispered, "I don't know how to describe it. It was a coughing kind of noise."

I sighed and hugged my knees, wishing Benita would go away. I'd probably never get back to sleep after the scare she had given me, but I didn't feel like spending the night baby-sitting her. "There's nothing unusual about someone coughing."

"It didn't seem right."

I sighed. "Did you hear anything else?"

She shook her head. "No. In spite of the

louvered doors, the rooms seem to be fairly well shielded from noise." She ducked her head a minute and I could hardly hear her add, "Of course I had my louvers firmly closed and locked."

"Then all you heard was a cough," I said.

"No. I said it was *like* a cough."

"Do you want to investigate?"

"Not by myself! Someone has to come with me."

"Okay," I said. "I will." I swung my legs out of bed and stood up, waiting for her to follow. Neither of us spoke as we walked as silently as we could down the veranda in our bare feet. We passed Benita's room. The doors were shut, but I could see light through the slits in the louvers.

I glanced toward it, and she whispered, "I was afraid that I wouldn't be able to turn the lantern on again, once I'd turned it off, so I just left it on."

I held a finger up to my lip and paused by the doors on the other side of Benita's room. The louvers were tightly shut. Just as she stepped up beside me we heard the door to the hallway open and shut. She gave a start and clutched my arm.

"If you want to ask Norton about his cough, you can probably find him downstairs," I said, and peeled her fingers from my arm.

"I—I feel a little silly," she stammered.

"Forget it. We're all pretty jumpy."

I turned and walked to the doors of her room and waited. Breathlessly she murmured, "Would you like to come in and visit a little while?"

"No, thanks," I said. "I want to get back to sleep."

"You're sure everything is all right?" she asked.

"It has to be."

She looked like a small child prepared to fight dragons in the dark as she threw open one of the doors and disappeared into the flat, yellow light. Quickly she shut the door, and I could hear the lock slip into place.

In panic I realized that I was standing alone in the dark and ran back to my room, resisting the temptation to bolt the outside doors as Benita had done. I tried to sleep, but wooden houses move and stretch in the night like the shades of old dinosaurs with aching bones, and I heard every sound.

Soon the sky lightened to gray, and then to a pale, clear, cloudless blue. I got up and pulled on my still-damp swimsuit, shivering as it stretched over my bed-warm skin. I tossed on a shirt, buttoning it up to the neck, grabbed a towel and the fins Ellison had lent me, and hurried out to the beach.

I met no one in the house and no one outside. I kept my back to the house just in case someone was watching as I unfastened my shirt and dropped it on the dock. The towel I took with me, draping it around my neck, over the ribbon. I quickly eased into the water, still surprisingly warm, and pulled on the fins. I needed those fins for speed, especially since the weight of the towel would hold me back.

As fast as I could swim I headed west, rounding the point, glad when I caught sight of the limestone promontory. The tide was up, so I dived more deeply to swim under the arch and from there into the cave. I climbed up on the ledge, took off my fins, and wrung as much water as I could out of the towel.

Walking gingerly on the rough limestone, I found a perfect niche deep in one of the near ledges. I took off the topaz, trying to keep my eyes from those of the monkey with the sharp golden paws, and wrapped it in the towel. I was taking no chances of having the artifact slip into a crevice in the rock or having some hermit crab scuttle away with it. Firmly I wedged the package into the niche and checked it carefully, finally satisfied that the artifact would be safe.

I made my way to the edge, tugged on my fins again, and jumped into the water.

On the way back to the dock I didn't take time to enjoy the undersea color. I suppose I didn't even notice it. I was relieved that the artifact was in a place where no one would find it, and reluctant to go back to face the others. The murderer— and it was a pretty sure thing that the judge had been murdered—was still in the house, but none of us had any idea who he could be.

He, I thought. *Why do I keep saying "he"?* There were three women in the group who could be suspect. No, two. I knew I wasn't the murderer, and surely Aunt Madelyn couldn't be. Benita seemed to be the most upset by the whole thing. She couldn't be the murderer—unless she was putting on an act, which was entirely possible.

As I swam I tried to think about each of the people in the judge's party. None of them looked or acted like a murderer, but one of them was. In movies or on television they cast people with sneaky, ferretlike faces or gorillalike bodies to play the villains, and they have cruel, deep-set eyes. It's easy to tell the bad guys from the good guys. Why couldn't life be that easy to figure out?

I climbed up on the dock, again shaking the water out of my hair, pulled on my shirt, and headed for the house. Benita, wearing a sundress, was seated in one of the wicker rockers on the lower veranda, drinking steaming coffee and fanning herself vigorously as little beads of sweat popped out on her forehead and upper lip.

"Have a nice swim?" she asked, as though our midnight conversation had never taken place.

"Great. The water is wonderful." I paused and added, "You seem to be feeling much better now."

"Well, of course I am," she snapped. "Last night — I suppose that everything seems more ominous at night. Besides, you're the one who insisted that everything was all right."

Maybe I had expected to be thanked for getting up in the night with her and allaying her fears. I should have known better.

"Where's your towel?" She put down her cup and looked at me quizzically.

"I should have brought one," I began, but she shook her head impatiently.

"You did. I saw you walk down to the dock about an hour ago, and you were carrying a towel."

"Darn!" I said, hoping that she couldn't see how her question had shaken me. "What happened to it?"

She shrugged. "It probably blew off the dock. Well, hurry in. You're not too late for breakfast."

Had I dreamed last night? I couldn't have. "How is Norton feeling this morning?"

"Norton? I have no idea. He hasn't come down for breakfast yet."

"You were worried about him last night."

She blinked with embarrassment. "I shouldn't have bothered you. Why do problems seem so much worse in the middle of the night?"

"Is everyone else up?" I asked.

She sighed. "I don't know. I really didn't feel like talking to anyone this morning." She hoisted herself out of the rocker. "I think I'll get another cup of coffee. Too much caffeine, but at a time like this, who cares?" She went inside.

I was still dripping, so I walked to the east end of the veranda and stood in the sun. And I felt that strange sensation again. I felt eyes upon me as distinctly as I could feel the dry tickle of drying salt water on my skin. I stared at the woods so intently, I thought I saw a bush move, a shadow fall back, but the feeling of being watched remained, so I turned and ran down the veranda, hurrying into the front door of the house.

After I had showered and changed to an old fun-run T-shirt and faded denim shorts, I went into the dining room to see what I could find to eat. Aldo and Kurt were sitting together. They stopped talking as I came in and greeted me somewhat glumly. *Tomorrow afternoon the boat will come back,* I told myself, *the police will be called, and eventually all of us here at the house will be able to get away from each other.*

On the sideboard was a large platter of Danish

rolls and cinnamon buns, a pitcher of orange juice, and a pot of coffee. I held up the coffeepot. "Did Ellison fix the generator?" I asked.

"Not yet," Kurt said, "but he's working on it. The coffee was made on the butane stove, and I'm afraid that it's getting a little cold."

I helped myself to some juice and rolls and took a seat across from Aldo.

"You had a swim," he said. "How was the water?"

Another watcher? Then I remembered that my hair was still damp. I suppressed a nervous giggle. "Beautiful," I said. "You ought to go for a swim. Ellison has all the snorkel equipment you'd need." I took a large bite of the Danish, squirting cherry glop on my chin.

At first, as I mopped off my face, I was angry at Aldo for laughing, but then he said. "You are so much like my daughter, Elizabeth. I remember her trying hard to be sophisticated and grown-up, then doing something like that—something a child would do."

"I'm sorry," I mumbled, then what he said penetrated. "You *remember* your daughter? I hope—"

"My wife and I were divorced five years ago, and my daughter lives with her mother in New Jersey," he said. "I see Elizabeth whenever I get a chance. Unfortunately, the pressures of my job are very demanding."

"Is it worth it?" I asked.

"If you were in business, you wouldn't ask that question," he said. "People have two lives, one in the business world, one in their own private world."

"It shouldn't have to be that way," I said.

Kurt butted in. "But it does. You're too young to understand."

I didn't answer, because I didn't agree with them.

Aldo sighed as he pushed back his chair. "I had promised Elizabeth I'd be on hand for her birthday party Sunday afternoon. Now I can't even inform her that my plans have changed."

As Aldo left the room Kurt poured himself another cup of coffee and sat down across from me.

"Did you sleep all right last night?"

"Not all night," I said. "Benita came into my room, because I'd left the veranda doors open. She wanted someone to talk to."

There was a slight change in his face, and I was glad I'd answered openly and truthfully, because he knew. "What did she want to talk about?" He took a long sip of coffee, staring down into the cup.

"She was worried about Norton," I said. "She heard something that frightened her."

He looked up quickly. "What?"

I laughed. "You won't believe it. She heard him cough."

"A cough? Is that all?"

"That's it. She was so frightened she was ready to jump at anything. I talked to her awhile and finally convinced her she should go back to bed, so she did."

He shook his head slowly. "She has a right to be

frightened. I feel so badly about all this. I think—I think I'd better try to make that swim."

"You can't do that." I leaned toward him eagerly. "Is there another boat on the island? Maybe some old sailboat or something? Anything that could float?"

"Not a thing," he answered.

Madelyn and Benita came into the room. Madelyn bent and kissed the top of my head.

"Would you like me to get some coffee for you?" I asked her.

"I've had breakfast, thanks," she said. "I was wondering—well, I just don't know what to do next. Maybe we should hold a meeting. They've all come down, haven't they?"

"Everyone except Norton," Kurt said. He looked at me and I knew we were thinking the same thing. "I'll check on him."

I was right behind him as he took the stairs two at a time, strode down the hall, and knocked at Norton's door. There was no answer. He tried the knob, and the door opened easily.

"He didn't lock it?" I asked.

But Kurt was pushing me back. I tried to peer over his shoulder, but he roughly shoved me aside and slammed the door in my face, yelling, "Stay out!"

Madelyn and Benita came running up the stairs. Aldo opened the door to his room and leaned out, staring at me quizzically.

"What is it?" he asked.

"I don't know," I answered.

Kurt opened the door and stepped into the hall,

closing it firmly behind him. He looked a little sick as he said, "The man is dead."

Benita began to tremble. "Are you going to tell us that Norton was murdered?"

"The man in that room isn't Norton Lindsay," Kurt began, but the rest of his sentence was drowned out as Benita threw herself into a full-blown case of hysterics.

CHAPTER

~~~~~~~~~~~~~~~~~~~~

8

It took all of us to get Benita back in control. I think it was Aldo's suggestion that we put her to bed and leave her alone to rest that stopped the wild tears.

"No!" Benita practically hung on Aunt Madelyn. "You can't leave me alone!"

"Then let's all go downstairs," Madelyn said as she tried to break Benita's grip. "You can lie on one of the sofas, Benita."

We managed to make it downstairs and deposited Benita on a sofa in the living room near one of the open veranda doors. For some reason—probably because Benita was being such a nuisance—I kept thinking of that line from *Hamlet,* "The lady doth protest too much, methinks."

The breeze carried the clean fragrance of sea salt and I breathed it in gratefully. We pulled chairs into a circle around Benita's sofa the way covered wagons once circled to protect themselves from the enemy outside. Except in this case there was no enemy outside. If we had an enemy, it had to be someone inside the circle.

I think we were all in shock. No one said a word as Kurt held out a wallet in one hand, some cards in another. "I tried to tell you when we were upstairs. The dead man wasn't Norton," he said. "What I mean is, the man we knew as Norton Lindsay wasn't Norton Lindsay, according to his driver's license and credit cards."

He paused and Aunt Madelyn said, "Well, go on. If he wasn't Norton, who was he?"

Kurt had the strangest expression on his face as he said, "Franklin Granakee."

"I can't believe that!" Madelyn gasped.

Kurt shrugged. "Have you ever met Granakee? Or seen a photo of him? Do you know what he looks like?"

"He doesn't allow himself to be photographed. Everyone knows that."

Kurt shoved the driver's license at her. As she studied the ID photo on it, her eyes widened. "Well," she said. She handed it back to Kurt, once more in command. "Could this be faked?"

"Why should it be?"

"Well, because—well, I have no idea." She didn't give up but looked at Kurt accusingly. "I distinctly remember Justin saying that you had thoroughly investigated every one of us."

"I did."

"Then why didn't you discover Norton's true identity?"

Kurt slumped back into his chair, looking both embarrassed and angry. "Why are you grilling me?" he snapped. "I check credentials all the way to the source. If the source is credible but is covering up, it's not my fault."

"Do you know who Mr. Malcolm represents?" I asked, but Aldo interrupted, so no one paid any attention to me.

As he reached for the cards and license to examine them, he said, "Mr. Granakee must have enjoyed posing at times as his own agent. It probably gave him greater freedom than if he had appeared as himself."

Benita spoke up, struggling among the pile of pillows to support herself on her elbows. "I can't believe it! Why should Franklin Granakee have wanted to pretend to be someone else? If we'd only known who he was, he would have been lionized!"

"I guess that's the reason," Madelyn said.

"But why did he die?" I asked.

"Isn't it obvious? He was murdered to get the artifact!" Benita's voice shook. Her eyes narrowed as she zeroed in on Madelyn. "We'll be killed off, one at a time! Whoever is hiding the artifact must give it up! Now!"

I shuddered and gripped the arms of my chair. I hadn't thought that someone would be killed because of what I had done. I felt sick, and the room became blurry. I'd get the artifact. I'd do it now. I squirmed to the edge of my chair, trying to make the dizziness go away before I got up. I'd hand the artifact over to the murderer. But which one in this room was the murderer?

Madelyn's cool, firm voice kept me in my chair.

"Calm down, Benita. We haven't got time for another case of hysterics. If we're going to reach correct solutions, we must think logically. I can't believe that Granakee was killed for the artifact. There was no reason for anyone to think he had the artifact. He showed no more sign of knowing its location than any of the rest of us."

"You may think that, but did his killer?" Benita's eyes were so wide and unblinking that it made my eyes itch to watch her.

Kurt broke in. "You didn't give me a chance to answer Madelyn's question, and you're way off the track. I told you he was dead. I didn't say anything about murder. He was just lying in bed like he died in his sleep. He was a nervous type. Maybe he had a heart attack."

"One more question," Madelyn said to Kurt, and I gave her points for reasoning more clearly than the rest of us. "Had Franklin Granakee's room been ransacked?"

"No," he said, frowning as he tried to remember. "Everything seemed to be in order. Granakee's clothes were folded and laid on a chair. His slacks, where I found the wallet, were draped over the back of the chair."

Aldo nodded toward the wallet, which had been laid on the coffee table. "Nothing seems to have been taken from his wallet."

"Of course not!" Benita rose indignantly, then flopped again. "None of us would stoop to thievery!"

"I think we should see the room," I said. They just stared at me, so I added, "Kurt is the only one

who's been in there, and we're just taking his word
for everything."

It didn't take them long to digest that. Almost
together they got up and went upstairs. I trailed
behind them. "Don't disturb anything," I called.
"The police—"

"That's enough," Madelyn said firmly, so I kept
my mouth closed and my eyes wide open.

Kurt had pulled the sheet up over Norton—
Granakee's face. Aldo pulled it down to study the
body, but I turned away. I'd give the police what
help I could, but I didn't want to look at another
dead body. For a few moments I just stood back
against the wall, hugging my arms and shivering. I
didn't want to be in this room any more than the
others did, but we had to do what was right, like it
or not. We didn't have a choice.

"He's just lying on his back, head on his pillow,"
Aldo said. In my peripheral vision I could see him
pull up the sheet again. I let out a long sigh of
relief.

Kurt had gone out on the veranda. Benita was
still on the landing. Madelyn and Aldo, murmur-
ing something to each other, left the room to join
Benita. For the first time I had a chance to get a
good look at the contents of the room. Nothing
looked suspicious or out of place, until I noticed
two small white feathers on the floor next to the
head of the bed. Another feather lay near the open
door.

Holding my breath, terrified of coming so close
to the body, I stepped to the side of the bed and
slid my fingers over and under the part of the

pillow that wasn't covered by the sheet. The underside of the pillow, near its edge, was torn. I lifted the pillow slip to get a better look. There were two small slits in the casing, from which other feathers were poking. One of the feathers fell to the floor as I examined the slits.

"Aunt Madelyn," I called, and she came to my side quickly. I guess I'd sounded as frantic as I felt. "Look at this," I said. "The pillow is ripped as though somebody's fingernails tore at it. It's like the pillow was over his face and he struggled and—"

Kurt stepped up beside me. "Some of the pillows are a little worn. See—the material is thin. There's a slit in my pillow too."

I straightened and faced him. "Could we see it?"

"Sure," he said easily. "Right now? Come on."

Madelyn put a hand on my arm. "Dramatic imaginings and wild accusations won't help."

"But—"

"Come downstairs," she said. "We'll all be more comfortable continuing the conversation there."

When we were all seated Madelyn was the first to speak. She said, "Again we are faced with the question of accidental death against murder. We don't know the answer."

"This wasn't supposed to happen!" Benita moaned.

"Control yourself, Benita," Aldo snapped.

"Let's be logical about this," Aunt Madelyn said. "Mr. Granakee's death could possibly have been from a heart attack. But it's necessary that we address the question of murder. *If* he was murdered, could it have been for a reason unrelated to the possession of the artifact?"

"Like what?" Kurt asked.

"He said he had seen Justin plug in the cord to the lamp. Maybe he saw something else. Or maybe someone thought that he had, and killed him for that reason."

A thought wiggled through my mind and darted out of it like the tiny yellow and blue fish that had sped under me in the cove. I tried to grab the thought, but I couldn't. Yet I knew in some way it was important.

Aldo shifted in his chair. "This is all guesswork. I think we should go back to facts. Maybe there is something else that Benita heard last night, some clue that might lead us to a greater knowledge of what happened to Franklin Granakee."

"No!" Benita screeched. "Nothing! I swear it!"

"But if you could be of help—"

"Don't push her," I said. "She really doesn't know anything else. My veranda doors were open, and she was frightened, so she came into my room to talk to me. She told me she heard Norton—uh—Mr. Granakee cough."

Benita groaned and pulled a pillow against her mouth.

"That's all she heard," I said. "I talked her out of being scared, and she went back to her own room to bed. That's it."

"There still may be something else, something she was unaware of at the time. If she thought hard about it—"

"Then she can tell the police when they get

here." I stood and shoved my chair out of the circle. "In case anyone's forgotten, someone in this house could be a murderer. Do you think that whoever it is will help us solve the crime?"

"Where are you going?" Madelyn asked.

"To get my camera," I said.

Kurt stood too. "No," he told me. "Let me take the photos. You've already found out that it's a disagreeable job. Where is your camera? I'll get it."

"Thanks," I said, and gave a loud sigh of relief. "The camera is on my chest of drawers," I answered, ignoring Benita's muffled sob. I moved toward the veranda. "I'm going to walk on the beach for a while and try to think."

"I should come with you," Madelyn said, but Benita tugged her down.

"I really do want to be by myself for a little while," I told her. "Besides, I think it would work out better if you and Benita stayed together."

I trotted down to the beach. I had swum toward the west. I'd walk toward the east. The hot sand filtered in and out of my sandals, and occasionally I kicked at a large seed pod that had fallen from one of the trees or jumped over a fallen branch or piece of washed-up driftwood. I tried to capture the thought that had eluded me, going over and over the conversation, but nothing helped.

I was well out of sight of the house when I got that weird, prickly feeling again and knew that someone was watching. I stopped and looked back along the beach, but no one had followed me. I walked a little farther, all my senses as taut as a guitar string ready to pop. The unseen eyes were still on me, and I could hear the quiet rustling of grasses and the not-so-quiet snap of a stepped-upon twig.

I whirled to face the sound and picked up a short chunk of bleached driftwood that lay near my feet. "Who are you?" I yelled. "Kurt? Ellison? Get out of there and stop spying on me!"

"Will you shut up?" someone hissed, and a face poked out of the bushes.

I was so surprised that I dropped my weapon. I was looking at a sun-bleached, sunburned guy who was probably not much older than I. He jumped out of the underbrush onto the sand, and I quickly scooped up the driftwood stick again, holding it high. He wore only torn cutoffs and ragged-looking deck shoes.

"Hey," he said, holding both palms up in a peace sign. "I'm not going to hurt you."

"Who are you?" I asked as I lowered the driftwood.

He looked down the empty beach in the direction from which I'd come and seemed satisfied. He sat on a large chunk of driftwood and said, "My name's Pete Michaels."

"What are you doing on this island?"

"Lying offshore."

"You're what?"

"I anchored my sailboat in a cove, girl."

"I've got a name," I said, "and it isn't 'girl.' It's Andrea Ryan."

"I bet that everyone calls you Andy," he said.

I studied him carefully. Surely he wouldn't have

nad the reason or the opportunity to have murdered Judge Arlington-Hughes or Norton—uh—Franklin Granakee. I didn't think I had to be afraid of him.

It was a delayed reaction, a real Three Stooges double take. I suddenly dropped the driftwood and gasped, "Pete! You have a boat!"

"I knew it would thrill you, once the idea sank in," he said.

"No! You don't understand! We need a boat to get off this island!"

"What happened to the one you came in?"

"It won't be back until late tomorrow afternoon."

"And you've got a heavy date tonight back in the States. Sorry. My boat's out of commission."

I dropped down on the driftwood next to him and rested my elbows on my knees, my head in my hands. He leaned over, looking up into my face. "Won't I do?" he asked. "You could tuck a flower in your hair, and I could hum something out of tune, and we could dance."

I had to smile. Pete was a nut, but I liked his sense of humor. I wished that Rick could loosen up like this once in a while. I pushed Rick out of my mind, sat up, and said, "There are a lot of blanks to fill in. Why don't you go first? Tell me how you happen to be on this island."

"Okay," Pete said. "It's a short, sad story. I was looking for a place to anchor and trying to beat some threatening squalls that were moving my way, and what do you know, the wire from the wheel to the rudder snapped, and I didn't have a spare to replace it, so . . ." He broke off. "I told you, this is a sad story. Could you look a little more sympathetic?"

"Can you still sail your boat?"

"Not with any accuracy."

"Then I am sorry," I said. "You don't know how sorry. Where's your sailboat now?"

"I managed to make it into a cove, pulled up the centerboard, and anchored it. It was dark by then, so I went to sleep."

"That's all? You just went to sleep?"

He shrugged. "What else? There weren't any good movies playing. Oh. Maybe I should mention that I'm not a morning person, so daylight kind of passed me by for a few hours. Next step was to scout around. At first I thought I was on a deserted island, but late in the afternoon I cut across to the north side and came across a house. Yeah! I said to myself. Maybe somebody there had a wire I could borrow. That's when I heard a motor and saw your boat pull up."

"You were the one who was watching me!" I said. "I could feel it."

"You're worth watching," he said, and continued without a pause. "Should I tell you about the judge?"

"You know him?"

"Unfortunately." He cocked his head and studied me. "You're not his daughter or niece or anything like that, are you?"

When I shook my head he said, "A month ago I went into Palm Beach to look around, and I was dressed like this. I guess I should have worn a tie, because I got picked up for vagrancy." He shook his head sadly. "Last year I had an old sorehead math teacher who didn't have a sense of humor and brought charges against us just because we hot-wired his car and left it on the lawn in front of the courthouse. So when Judge Arlington-Hughes was told I had a record, he let me sit in jail all night, then read me the riot act. I'd probably be there yet, except I kept demanding that I be allowed to call my father, who's a big-shot lawyer in Miami."

He paused and said, "Look, Andy, I didn't say I had class. Okay?"

"I'd probably do the same thing," I said. "Anyhow, you hadn't committed any crimes. You shouldn't have gone to jail."

"Yeah," he said, and smiled. "When I saw you I knew we'd think the same way about things." He paused. "I'm not a bad guy, Andy. If you talked to my mom, she'd tell you."

"I didn't ask for a reference," I said. "Go on with your story."

"Okay. That private eye-muscleman who works for the judge knew my dad and said I was who I claimed I was, so they just told me to get out of town. The PI, who ought to get picked up for carrying a concealed weapon, escorted me to the city limits and kicked me across the invisible line."

"That's terrible!" I said.

"Yeah, so when I saw the two of them get off that boat—"

"The private eye? He wasn't on the boat."

"Sure he was. Tall, dark-haired, looks like a football player. His name's Frank Bartley."

I stood up, trying to sort all this out. "There's someone who looks like that who works for the judge, but he's a secretary, and his name is Kurt Cameron."

Pete got up, too, standing so close to me that I could feel the warmth from his arm next to mine "Secretary? That's what he calls himself? Don't believe it. Ha! Don't believe anything he tells you."

CHAPTER

~~~~~~~~~~~~~~~~~

9

"But my Aunt Madelyn knows him," I said.

"I bet she didn't know him in Miami," Pete said. "Bartley used to work there, and he did a couple of investigative jobs for my father. I recognized him."

"Why would he use another name?"

"Private investigators use aliases all the time. Fake jobs, fake business cards, you name it—fake. Maybe he used the name of Kurt Whatever when he worked jobs for the judge so people wouldn't find out he's a PI. A secretary stays in the background, right? Nobody wonders about a secretary."

I thought about it a minute. Pete was probably right. "Do you want to come to the house and see if Ellison can find the wire you need to fix your boat?" I asked him.

"Not with the judge and the muscleman there," he said.

Of course. He didn't know. So I filled him in on

everything that had happened. Well, not exactly everything, because I didn't tell him that I had taken the artifact.

When I finished he let out a long, low whistle. "No wonder you want to get off this island," he said. "I'm with you. How good are you at the dog paddle?"

I must have looked awfully discouraged, because Pete took my hand and said, "Come on. I'll cheer you up. I'll show you my boat."

He led me along a natural path among the trees, and I could see that the woods were crisscrossed with these grassy open strips and spots. In some places we had to push away branches or vines, but the going wasn't difficult. The island was narrower than I thought, so it didn't take us long to reach the small cove where Pete's boat was anchored.

It was a beautiful little boat, about twenty-five feet long, with a tiny cabin. Pete waded to one side of the boat. The water was about hip deep where he stood. "If you don't mind getting wet, you can come aboard. But keep your shoes on. There are some spiny things just under the water here that you shouldn't step on with bare feet."

I didn't mind getting wet. I was curious. I followed him up the aluminum ladder to the deck.

"The wheel's out here," Pete said, "but take a look below. That's where I live."

I leaned in to see a tiny cabin that was laid out with a padded bench on one side, a table over a compact ice chest, stove, and sink on the other side. "Tucked up in the bow is my bed," Pete said, "and beyond the door at the side is the head.

Would you like something to eat?" He jumped down into the cabin, opened the nearest cupboard, and pulled out some packages of Twinkies. I climbed down the short flight of steps and sat on the padded bench.

"Do you cook?" I asked.

"Sure. Anything that comes in a can. I'm self-sufficient."

He sat next to me. We split a package of Twinkies and drank some warm cola. "Ice melted," Pete explained.

"You are in a bad way," I told him. "Do you want to see if Ellison has got some tools so you can work on your rudder?"

"I've got tools," he said. "It's the wire that I need."

I stood up, nearly bumping my head on the low ceiling. "Why don't I look around for a wire? There must be a storeroom or shed or something where they'd keep things like that at the judge's house. Just show me what I'm supposed to be looking for."

Pete frowned. "That's out of the question. Too risky." He leaned across me, resting one arm on the doorframe, effectively blocking my way. "I don't like the idea of your going back there for any reason."

"Neither do I, but my aunt's there," I said. "Besides, if I don't show up, they'll probably come looking for me and find your boat."

"I shouldn't let you go to the house alone. I'll come with you."

"A stranger shows up on the island and two men

die. You know what the people at the house will think, especially because they don't like the idea that one of their group might be a murderer. They'll all be suspicious of you."

"Are you?"

I looked right into his eyes, but I couldn't read his thoughts. "I haven't any reason to be," I answered.

He straightened to let me pass, then followed me up on the deck. "Okay. Go back. You know where I am, and I'll be checking on you."

"Deal," I said.

"Do you know how to get back?"

"I ought to find the house if I keep heading west."

"It's a little longer, but a lot easier, if you just cut across to the beach on the other side," he said.

But I wanted the quickest route, so I headed through the woods. At first the going was easy, but thick patches of trees blocked the sky and the sun, and I had to guess a couple of times on my direction. The woods were quiet—too quiet. The silence was like a fog that crept after me, that would crawl over and smother me. Frantically, I deserted my plan to head west and made for the north beach, pushing through underbrush, scrabbling and tripping, until I broke clear, falling on my knees on the sand.

The sunlit water was so peaceful and beautiful that I felt like a fool, like Benita in her hysterics. I had let my imagination capture me, the way I had when I was four and was sure there was a monster under my bed. I sat on the sand for a few minutes, catching my breath, then followed the beach north until the judge's plantation house lay ahead, a foreboding blob of shadow in what should have been sun.

As I came toward the house I saw Ellison wiping his hands on a rag and heading toward the door to the kitchen. I ran up the front steps to the lower veranda and through the front door. Someone had left on a table lamp in the living room, and it cast a puddle of light. So Ellison had finally fixed the generator. Good. I felt much better knowing we'd have electric light tonight. I flipped off the lamp switch and went upstairs to my room.

Everything in my room looked the same as it had, so there was no reason for the creepy feeling that someone besides me had been in it. I checked the small closet, and my clothes were hanging where I had left them. Well, almost where I had left them. The bottom half of my pajamas was hanging on the hook over the top half, and I always hang up my pajamas with the top on top.

It was a shock to think that someone had searched my room. Then shock gave way to an anger so intense that the room took on a dull, reddish haze. How dare they!

I sat on the edge of the bed and tried to calm down. What could they have found? Nothing. I hadn't brought much with me. There wasn't much of anything in the room. The candlestick and candles and matches were still on the chest of drawers, next to my camera. My camera had been moved, but I had expected that because Kurt had used it.

I reached to pick up the camera and discovered that the back had been opened. Had Kurt used up the rest of the roll of film? No. I groaned in frustration and slammed one fist on top of the chest. The film was still in place. The back had been opened to expose the film. The whole roll was ruined.

Had Kurt done this? It didn't make sense. Why would he take the shots, then deliberately spoil them? Was his offer just his way of discovering the location of my camera and covering himself so that he could do this to the film?

Any of them—Aldo, Benita, Ellison, or even Aunt Madelyn—could have opened the back of my camera.

I closed it with a snap and walked out to the veranda, leaned on the railing, watched the brilliant sea, and fought the desire to curl up in ball and cry.

"It's unbelievable!" Benita's voice rose to a high, excited pitch. Her voice was coming from a room far down on the veranda, a room with the shutters wide open. If she was in that room, then Aunt Madelyn was probably with her. Maybe they could tell me something about my ruined film. Angrily, I strode down the veranda and stopped at the open doors.

Madelyn was on her hands and knees, searching under the single, double bed. Benita was pawing through the top drawer in a chest of drawers, and Aldo's back was toward me as he rummaged in the closet.

"He won't come back. I know it, I know it!" Benita was saying.

I stepped into the room and shouted at them, "What are you doing?"

They looked at me and froze, eyes wide like wild rabbits caught in headlights on the roadside at night.

"Whose room is this?" I asked. "Where's Kurt?"

Madelyn was the first to recover. She got to her feet and said, "Something has happened, Andrea."

"What?"

Benita stepped forward, like a kid wanting to tell a secret first. "We found Kurt's shoes and shirt on the dock. He told us earlier he was going to try to swim to the nearest inhabited island. So that's what he's done! We're sure of it!"

"He can't do that!"

"But he did."

I just stared at them for a moment as I tried to absorb the information. Then I remembered what they'd been doing. "I don't understand why you're searching his room," I said.

Madelyn said, "Be realistic, Andrea. You saw the artifact. It's priceless. We can't leave the island without it, so we must hunt until we find it."

"You searched my room, too, didn't you?"

Benita had the grace to look slightly embarrassed, but Aldo said, "We are all under suspicion."

"Then why don't we search *your* room?" I demanded.

"We did," Madelyn said.

"What did you find?"

"Nothing."

I remembered what Pete had told me about Kurt's real identity. Had they discovered that yet?

I glanced at the top of the chest and saw a set of car keys, a pocket comb, and a wrinkled handkerchief. "Where's his wallet?" I asked.

"We didn't find a wallet," Benita said. She looked indignant. "You don't understand. We're looking for the artifact only. We aren't prying into people's wallets, for goodness sakes!"

"Just into cameras."

"What are you talking about?" Madelyn asked.

"My film," I grumbled. "Someone opened the back of my camera and exposed the whole roll. All the pictures Kurt and I took have been ruined."

"Kurt didn't know how to use your camera. He said so," Madelyn explained. "Maybe while he was trying to figure out how it worked he accidentally opened the back plate."

An accident again? How often would that excuse be used? I kept my thoughts to myself and didn't answer.

Aldo swept the room with his gaze. "We're through in here," he said. "I suppose the next step will be a thorough search of the downstairs rooms."

"Come with us, Andrea," Madelyn said. "We need all the help we can get."

"Wait a minute," I said. "Hasn't it occurred to any of you that if someone finds the artifact, he— or she—isn't likely to let on? We could hunt all day, while the finder had it in his pocket."

It didn't rattle them. "We've made a pact," Benita said. "We're going to share the proceeds from the artifact."

"But that topaz isn't yours!" I said. "It wasn't the judge's property either."

Aldo looked puzzled. "I don't understand. Whose property is it?"

"It belongs to the country of Peru," I said. "It was smuggled out, and that's illegal."

He relaxed and even smiled.

"Oh, good heavens," Benita grumbled. "Is that all you're talking about." She walked into the hall, and the others followed.

I took the opportunity to pick up Kurt's pillow and examine it. No tear, no rip, no feathers falling through. He had lied to me, taking the chance that I wouldn't call him on it. Why? I dropped the pillow back on the bed and tried to think, but nothing added up.

"Are you coming, Andrea?" Madelyn called.

I went with them. I'd go through the motions of hunting for the artifact. It would give me time to think, and here was certainly another question to wonder about. Was I the only one who was puzzled about Kurt's missing wallet?

I assumed those were his clothes left rumpled on the floor, and Madelyn had said he had left his shoes on the beach. His wristwatch was probably waterproof. Not seeing a wristwatch in the room didn't bother me. But his wallet? A swimmer would never carry a wallet with him. What was Kurt up to? I didn't understand this at all. I badly needed to talk this over with someone. Not Aunt Madelyn. Not anyone in this house. The only person on this island I could talk to would be Pete.

Ellison served ham and cheese sandwiches for

lunch. He'd made too many, so as the others left
the dining room I wrapped up a couple of sandwiches in a paper napkin and managed to slip
through the kitchen and out the back door without anybody noticing me.

I didn't go down to the beach. I'd be too visible.
I followed the shoreline as I traveled through the
woods, trying to find the spot at which we'd cut
across to the other side of the island.

I made a couple of wrong guesses before I found
a path that looked familiar. Confident now, I followed it over a rise and emerged at the little cove.
Pete was bent over the boat's rudder.

"Hi," I said.

He started so violently that he almost tumbled
overboard. He managed to straighten and said, "I
didn't hear you coming."

"I didn't mean to scare you."

"Didn't you? When we first meet you threaten
me with a stick. Then you tell me about a couple of
murders and a murderer loose on the island. And
you don't mean to scare me?"

I laughed and held up my package. "I brought
you something to eat."

"Great. Food is always welcome."

As we sat on deck and he demolished the sandwiches, I told him about Kurt.

"That guy wouldn't be self-sacrificing enough to
try to swim for help. And he's no dummy. He
knows the odds. He'd never make it. If he didn't
sink from exhaustion, he'd probably get attacked
by a shark." Pete licked his fingers and shook his
head. "Nice lunch. Thanks for thinking about me."

Before I could answer he leaned over and kissed me softly, warmly on the lips.

I scrambled up quickly and walked a few steps away from him. I had liked his kiss, and that bothered me, because it made me feel disloyal to Rick. *Go away,* I wanted to yell at Pete. *I've got enough problems to worry about!*

Pete just leaned back on his elbows, as though the kiss hadn't happened, and said, "As I see it, the big question to answer is, who's got the artifact?"

"Why? I thought we were talking about Kurt."

"We can talk about anybody we want to, but we've got to get down to the most important issue. I think your aunt is right that the judge wasn't murdered for the artifact. It would have been easy for someone to get it away from him without killing him. And that other guy who was murdered—if it was murder—I doubt if that would have been for the artifact either."

I gasped aloud as I remembered. "It *was* murder."

"I thought you said no one was sure."

"I know what I said, because I didn't remember then, but I do now. I walked down the veranda with Benita, and we stood outside Norton's—Mr. Granakee's—room, and we heard his door to the hallway open and close."

"Maybe it was before he was murdered."

"No." I shook my head. "I'm sure of what happened. He must have been smothered. That's when Benita heard what she thought was a cough. He must have fought back, because his fingernails tore the pillow casing. The murderer probably put the room back in order again—or even took time to search it before we got there. We heard him leaving the room."

"Whew!" Pete said. "I don't like that. If you're right, things aren't going to get any better. They're going to get worse."

"What do you mean?" I sat on the bench across from him and leaned forward intently. Wavelets rocked the boat in a rhythmic motion, and the sun was warm on my back, but I couldn't relax.

"Because time is running out. The boat will come back tomorrow afternoon. The artifact has to be found by then, and one of those people at the house is going to want it badly enough to do anything to get hold of it. Whoever knows where it's hidden is probably in a lot more danger than that person suspects."

"That person is me," I said in a small voice. I was as surprised at telling him my secret as he was at hearing it.

He opened his mouth a couple of times before anything came out. "Why?"

"Because I have to return it to Peru," I said, and proceeded to tell him what Dr. Sammy Kirschman had told us about how wrong it was to steal a country's artifacts and how strongly I agreed with him.

When I'd finished he rubbed his chin and said, "That thing could be worth an awful lot of money. I mean, what do you want? College? A Porsche? College *and* a Porsche?"

"Don't joke about it. All I want is to make sure it gets back where it belongs."

He studied me a minute, head tilted. "This is an interesting side to your character, which, so far during the years we have known each other, has never emerged. Andy Ryan, girl crusader."

I began to tense, wishing I hadn't told him. "Are you making fun of me?"

"Oh, no, Andy." Pete crossed to sit next to me and took my hands in his. "I kid around with people I like, that's all. And I like you very much. I was trying to be funny. I didn't mean anything else, honest."

I sighed with relief. I couldn't help it.

"And I didn't mean to scare you," he added. "I guess now we're both scared. I don't like to think about you being the one in the tight spot."

"I'll be all right," I said. "They don't know I have the artifact."

"You shouldn't have it on your person. It's too dangerous. I tell you what, give it to me, and I'll hide it here on the boat for you."

"I'm not wearing it," I said.

He shook his head. "I hope you really hid it good, because, from what you told me, they're likely to take the house apart looking for it. It is at the house, isn't it?"

"Does it matter?" I asked.

"It matters to me," he said. "Andy, we're dealing with a murderer." His voice became softer as he moved a little closer and added, "I want you to trust me."

Nervously, I squirmed back a couple of inches. I pulled my hands from his.

Pete didn't act as I expected him to. He folded

his arms across his chest and said, "This is not a very good beginning for a friendship. Someday we'll laugh about this, but right now we keep scaring each other."

"I'm not afraid of you."

"You're giving a good imitation. Hey, it's my fault. I probably got too intense about wanting to protect you. Believe me, Andy, I was just trying to help, that's all."

"That college and Porsche bit," I said. "You sounded as though you could go for that too."

"Me? Those are the very things I'm temporarily trying to escape." He smiled and added, "Money doesn't mean anything to me. Just ask my dad. In fact, those were the exact words he used during our last argument."

I couldn't leave it alone. "It must take money to travel the way you're doing it."

He nodded. "I'm living on a very small amount I took from a generous trust fund my grandfather left for me. I wish he hadn't. He earned it, and I wish he'd spent it all on himself." He looked away from me for a moment and said, "You probably think of me as a spoiled beach bum. You're in good company. That's how my father sees me too."

"Oh, no," I mumbled, but Pete shrugged and tried to smile.

"I just wanted a year to myself," he said, "before I got onto the treadmill of college and law school and joining my father's firm."

For the first time since I'd met him, his eyes were serious. I'd hurt him, and it made me feel terrible. "I'm sorry, Pete." I stood, and Pete stood, too, facing me. "It's hard for me to trust," I told him, "because—well, there is—was—a guy I trusted, but we had an argument and broke up. He's—uh—temporarily dating someone else."

"If he broke up with you to date someone else, even temporarily, then he's an idiot," Pete said. His arms slid from my shoulders to wrap tightly around me, and his kiss, as warm as the sunlight, tasted of salt water.

To make amends for all that I'd said, naturally I kissed him in return, and my knees were a little shaky when I finally pulled away and murmured, "I'll try to bring you some dinner this evening."

"Don't take any chances," he said. "I've got plenty of cold canned beans and Twinkies. At the last grocery store I visited I got a really good buy on Twinkies."

"I'll see you later," I said.

Pete waved to me when I turned, just before I entered the grove of trees, and as I walked along the path I smiled, thinking about the funny things he had said. Pete was so different from Rick.

I wished I hadn't thought about Rick, because a smidgen of guilt came back, just enough to make me uncomfortable. Pete was a guy I'd see tomorrow, then never see again. Rick was real. He had been a big part of my life, and I couldn't believe it was over. I'd made promises to Rick, and he'd made promises to me. Surely those promises couldn't be broken so easily. "Grow up," he had told me, because he didn't understand. Maybe it was all my fault. Maybe I was the one who couldn't understand. Never mind what had happened.

When I was home and could talk to him, we'd solve our problems. No matter what Mom had said, Rick would be part of my life again.

The trailing end of a vine slapped my face, and I ducked, pushing it aside. I hadn't been paying attention to where I'd been going, and now where was I? It certainly wasn't the path to the north beach.

Ahead of me was another clearing, so I worked my way through. I wouldn't let myself think about being lost on this island because then I'd be afraid. I held my imagination in tightly, as though it were on a chain. Not a call of a bird, not the splash of the sea. The silence moved in, smothering me.

I raced along the cleared path as fast as I could manage without tripping and falling flat on my face. I scratched my arms against branches and the rough trunks of palms, and beat back waving tendrils of vines. I lost all sense of direction. I kept telling myself that the island wasn't that large, that Pete's cove was close enough to the house to begin with. I couldn't be too far from it, but once again I was on the verge of panic.

Suddenly the clearing widened, and at the edge of it was a row of palms, facing the sea. I ran ahead, grasping one of the rough trunks for support, and gaped at the cove that lay below me. Anchored in the cove was a good-sized powerboat!

It was smaller than the judge's powerboat, *Croesus,* not big enough to need a crew, but it looked as though it could easily carry five or six people. I couldn't believe such good luck! Was the owner of this boat someone like Pete who had wandered in, looking for a place to anchor?

The slope was gentle, so I scrambled down easily to the beach. I wasn't quiet. I didn't want to startle anyone. In fact, I hoped that someone would come up from the cabin.

"Anybody here?" I called as I waded out into the water. "Hello? Anyone around?"

A ladder hung over the side. I gripped it and hoisted myself up on the deck just as the door to the cabin opened, and someone came up the stairs.

"Well, well. Andrea," Kurt Cameron said. "What do you think you're doing here?"

CHAPTER

〰〰〰〰〰〰

10

For the second or two I must have gone blank, because I suddenly became aware that Kurt was gripping my shoulders and gently shaking me. "Snap out of it, Andrea!" he said. "Don't do something stupid like fainting."

I opened my eyes. "I won't. Stop shaking me."

He looked concerned. "You'd better sit down." He propelled me against the padded bench on deck. When the back of my legs hit it he let go, and I flopped.

For a few moments we just looked at each other. I wondered what I was supposed to say. I couldn't think of anything clever that would get me out of this mess, so I blurted out, "So—there were no boats on the island. And you're supposed to be taking a five-mile swim to get help."

"Is that what they believe?"

"That's what you led them to believe."

He leaned forward, resting his elbows on his

knees, and said, "Andrea, two men have been murdered."

I interrupted. "I thought we didn't know for sure."

"I do know. I'm sure. I saw the same evidence that you saw."

"This is making me angry!" I said. "All this sneaking and hiding and pretending and—"

"Listen to me," Kurt said. "I'm not Judge Arlington-Hughes's secretary. I'm a private investigator."

My mouth opened and shut and opened again like those big-eyed fish in an aquarium. Nothing came out. Pete was right. And Kurt had actually told me.

"I had to get away from the others to think things out. It's up to me to investigate this case."

I held out my hands toward the boat. "Why didn't you use this to go for help?"

"And leave somebody else to get murdered?" He shook his head. "No way."

"Aunt Madelyn said that the judge and Mr. Granakee weren't killed for the artifact."

He shrugged. "We don't really know why they were murdered. But it's a sure thing that the killer wants to get hold of the artifact before that boat comes tomorrow afternoon."

"They told me they were going to share it," I said.

He raised one eyebrow questioningly. "Do you trust them?"

"I trust my aunt."

"Do you?"

I shivered. "Do you have a radio on the boat? Could we call out for help?"

"No radio," he said. "The boat isn't big enough to need one."

"Then teach me how to use this boat. You can stay here and protect everyone while I go for help."

"No. You don't know these islands or the way to Freeport."

"You could teach me that too."

"It's too much to learn in too short a time."

"If someone . . ." I almost told him about Pete, but a dark shiver at the back of my mind stopped me. Kurt was waiting for what I'd say next, so I babbled, "Does someone else, like Ellison, know about this boat?"

"He knows about the boat, but he doesn't know it's on the island."

"Whose boat is it?"

"The judge's."

"Then shouldn't it be tied up at his dock?"

"Remember his plan? He wanted everyone kept on the island until the bidding for the artifact was over."

"Oh." I did remember. That made sense. I had no more questions to ask.

"I didn't expect anyone to go exploring this far," Kurt said. "How did you find this cove?"

"I went into the woods and got lost."

"Do you remember your way back?"

I shook my head, then realized what he had just said. "You're going to let me go?"

"If I do, you know that you've got to keep quiet about this boat being here."

I just stared at him for a moment, and he added, "I'm not asking. I'm ordering. Look, Andrea, you can figure out that if I hold you here on the boat, the others will come searching for you and probably stumble on it the way you did. On the other hand, I can't have you ruin my investigation."

His voice became a patronizing pat on the head. "You're a smart girl. Maybe you can even help me with the investigation."

I was smart enough to know I'd better cooperate with him. Even though he'd told me his real occupation, I didn't trust him any more than I did the others, but I nodded. "What do you want me to do?"

"Pay attention to what is said and done. Listen carefully. Between the two of us we ought to be able to pick up on anything that doesn't seem right."

I guess I looked a little dubious, because he added, "And do what you can to find the artifact. Somebody's hidden it. I'd give anything to know who took it. Or where it is." He scowled at his own thoughts. "If you find it, bring it to me right away —to *me* and nobody else."

"Okay," I said quickly. I stood up.

Kurt stood, too, blocking my way. I realized again what a big guy he was. "You've got to promise you won't tell the others about the boat."

"I promise," I answered quickly. I could keep that promise, because "the others" didn't include Pete.

"Then go back to the house," he said. "Don't mention that you saw me. I'll be along in a while. There are a couple of things I have to do here first."

"What are you going to tell them?"

He shrugged. "That I went exploring on the island, hoping to find some way of going for help. Only there wasn't anything to find. No luck." He looked pleased with himself. "That should keep anyone else from feeling desperate enough to try to explore the island."

Kurt stepped aside, and I walked to the back of the boat, swinging my legs over the side, and jumped, landing hip deep in the water.

"Remember the promise," he said. "Because if you don't keep it . . ."

He didn't finish the sentence. I could recognize a threat when I heard it. I just nodded and waded as fast as I could to the shore, calling, "How do I get back to the house?"

"Through the woods," he said. "Cut across to the north beach. The island's not that big. You'll find it."

He grinned as I stumbled into the woods. My sandals squished, my shorts dripped water that ran down my legs, and I had so much to think about this time that I wasn't frightened of the silent woods themselves. I tried to head north, and in a short time found myself staring through the rim of trees at the beach. The house was close by on the left. I couldn't be sure that Kurt hadn't followed me, so I ran to the house and up the stairs and changed my clothes.

I didn't know what to think about Kurt. He'd been honest about being a private investigator. I supposed he felt compelled to protect us too. I did wonder about his interest in the artifact, though. Maybe the missing artifact was his real reason for hanging around.

It didn't matter. What mattered was that he was in possession of a powerboat, and I was sure that Pete would know how to handle that boat, just given the chance.

I came downstairs as silently as I could, which wasn't very, since the wooden stairs creaked and popped with each step. I could hear voices, so I tiptoed in my cold, wet sandals through the living room to the dining room. The three of them were in the kitchen questioning Ellison, and from the occasional banging of pots and rattle of dishes, I could tell they had expanded their search for the artifact. Good. That should keep them busy for a while. I hoped they wouldn't miss me.

I had intended to jog in the wet sand along the north beach until I came to the place where I should cut across to the other side of the island and Pete's cove. The tide was out, and the sand was soaked and shiny, little air bubbles emerging from the tiny holes made by submerged sea creatures, the bubbles blurping and popping like damp fireworks. But I had gone only a short distance when I could feel someone's presence. Someone was watching me.

Stopping short, I turned in a half circle, first to look down the beach behind me where the house was completely hidden by a curved peninsula of trees, scrub, and sand, then to the woods. Someone from the house could have tracked me. Or it could be Kurt, or—

A voice hissed at me from the trees. "Is it safe to come out?"

Or Pete.

"How long have you been following me?" I demanded as Pete cautiously climbed over a small shrub and jumped to the sand.

"I thought you were following me." He smiled wickedly, but when I didn't smile in return he said, "Andy, I told you I was going to keep an eye on you."

"You're supposed to be taking care of your boat."

"There's nothing much I can do to the boat."

"How long have you been watching me?"

"Not long. First I watched the house. Then I saw you come out."

"Why didn't you say something?"

"I wanted to make sure that no one was going to come after you." He smiled again. "You didn't happen to bring anything else to eat, did you?"

"No," I said, "I came to tell you something important, so be serious."

"Okay," he said, and dropped to a cross-legged position on the sand. "Tell me. I'm listening."

I told him about Kurt and the boat.

Pete jumped up and hit one fist into the palm of his other hand. "I warned you about that guy, didn't I?"

"I don't know what to think about him, Pete. He did tell me the truth about being a private eye."

"Did you believe that stuff about his having to investigate?"

"That's what investigators are supposed to do— investigate, isn't it?"

"Well, yeah, I suppose so," he said grudgingly, "but I still don't trust him."

"I don't think I do either," I said. "But we have to give him the benefit of the doubt."

"Why?"

"Because what if Kurt really is working honestly to protect us and uncover the murderer? We wouldn't want to accidentally do anything to ruin his plans for him. Besides, I promised not to tell anyone at the house about the powerboat."

"You don't have to keep a promise like that."

"Yes, I do," I said, "unless I find a very good reason not to."

"You're unreal!" Pete muttered. He looked at me carefully. "Let me get things straight. Why did you tell me about the boat?"

"So you could steal it."

"What?" He gave such a start that he staggered to one side, nearly falling over an exposed tree root. I hung on, helping him keep his balance. Once recovered, he shook his head slowly. "You won't break a promise, but you'd steal a boat."

"It's not like that," I said. "What I mean is, we have to give Kurt a chance to prove that he's telling the truth. But if he isn't, then we might need the boat to go for help. Do you understand the difference?"

"Unfortunately, I do," he said.

"Do you know how to run a powerboat?"

"Sure."

"So if I decide that—"

"You're making the rules?" he asked.

"I have to, Pete. I have to be fair."

"Okay," he said, and headed into the woods.

"Where are you going?" I asked.

"You mean, where are *we* going? We're going to find this cove so that you can show me the boat. Come on!"

He held out a hand, so I staggered through the sand to grab it and followed him into the shadows under the trees.

His hand was warm and strong, and I held it tightly. He tried to follow a clearing or two before he was satisfied that we were heading in the right direction.

"How can you tell?" I asked.

"If you sail a lot, you get pretty good at judging directions."

"You missed the first couple of tries."

"You weren't supposed to notice."

I tugged on his hand, pulling him to a stop. "Pete," I said, "we'll have to be careful that Kurt doesn't see us or hear us. I'm a little bit afraid of him."

"Then you're braver than I am," he said. "I'm a whole lot afraid of him. Remember that, being a PI, he probably carries a gun."

"So far you haven't been involved in any of our troubles, because no one but me knows you're on the island. I guess I shouldn't have involved you now."

"No guilt feelings," he said. "Look at it from my

point of view. There I sat with a rudder out of commission. I don't have a radio to call for help. I could have been marooned for weeks, eating Twinkies until I figured out a way to repair that wire. I admit that I'm not too crazy about getting mixed up with a possible murderer, but on the other hand I met you, and you found a boat for me. Us," he amended quickly, adding after only a short pause, "which we will use only on your orders and in case of dire emergency."

His face crinkled in a grin, and he looked like a mischievous ten-year-old as he said, "The best part of the whole deal is you, of course. Men have dreamed of landing on a tropical beach and finding a beautiful girl." I couldn't help smiling at him. I had to admit to myself that he wasn't the only one who was glad that we'd met.

"Let's move as quietly as possible," he said, "and no more talking. If you want to whisper something, just tug on my hand."

I thought he was still being funny, so I was amazed to find, after just a few more steps, that the clearing we'd been following began to look familiar. It spread out to the top of a rise that was rimmed with palms and some low bushes.

Pete made a downward motion with his hand, so I followed his lead and dropped, crawling toward the row of palms. He lay on his stomach, barely parting the bushes, and I lay beside him.

"There she is," he whispered. "And isn't she super-looking?"

"Who?" I stared through a part in the leaves, but

all I could see was the boat rocking gently in the water.

"Boats are always referred to as 'she,' " he whispered.

We watched for a few minutes. "Kurt doesn't seem to be around," Pete said. "Maybe we could go down for a closer look."

I put a hand on his arm to hold him back. "No! I did that, and Kurt appeared out of nowhere. We can't take the chance."

"He said he'd be going back to the house soon."

"But we don't know if he has yet," I argued. "We'd have to keep watch on the boat and see him actually leave."

"I suppose you're right," he murmured.

We watched a few minutes longer, and I asked, "Do you know how to use a boat like that?"

"Sure," he said. "It's not hard. You turn on the engine with a key and steer it the way you would a car. It's got a throttle, and you can set the speed."

"With a key," I repeated.

He nodded. "I thought about that."

"Would the key be kept on the boat?"

"We wouldn't know that unless we went down to look. He might keep it on the boat, and he might keep it on his person." I guess my fingers tightened on his arm, because he patted my hand and said, "You're right about not just blundering in. We're too smart to take unnecessary chances."

"How are we going to find out?"

"I'll check out the boat this afternoon. If I'm sure that Kurt isn't around, I'll search for the key."

"Promise me you'll be careful," I whispered.

"Promises, promises," he said. "You bet I'll promise."

"We'd better leave now," I said.

He sidled backward, so that when he stood he couldn't be seen from the cove. "Come on. I'll walk you home."

I joined him, and he easily led me back the way we had come. I would have become lost again, but traveling through these woods seemed so easy for Pete.

"Well, well," Pete said as we caught sight of the house. "There's old bigfoot now, and it looks like he's really getting it." Kurt was on the lawn with Benita, standing up fairly well to what was obviously a tirade on her part.

Pete gave me a quick good-bye. I didn't turn to watch him leave. I knew he'd be going back to search the boat, and even though Kurt was here and wouldn't discover him, the whole idea frightened me. I didn't want anything to happen to Pete. I ran toward the house, ignoring the others, and sat on the veranda steps, watching the sun melt into gold and burn the western sky with violent, deep red scars.

Dinner was awful. Ellison wouldn't go near the freezer so we ate whatever was left over in the refrigerator and pantry. His cooking had definitely gone from bad to worse. The atmosphere in the dining room was horrible too. Everyone was more angry that Kurt hadn't made the swim for help than they were relieved that he hadn't taken such a desperate chance. Suspicion was thicker than

Ellison's gravy, and everyone shared the same, miserable mood.

"Nobody found the artifact?" My words came out more like a statement than a question.

Aunt Madelyn glowered at me. "You could have stayed to help search for it."

"Yes," Benita complained. "It was hard work. Why did you think you were excused?"

"Oh," I said, and found I didn't have an answer. "I didn't think you really needed me to help."

"We did. Kurt could have helped too." Benita sighed. "We have searched the entire house, and I, for one, don't know where else to look."

Kurt put down his water glass. "I'm afraid we're down to a personal search," he said.

"That's unthinkable," Madelyn snapped.

"Is it? There are only two places the artifact could be—hidden in the house or on someone's person."

"But that's an invasion of privacy," Madelyn said.

"Maybe so, but it comes down to this—do you want the artifact or don't you?"

Aldo stood up. "I think we should make it possible for Ellison to clear the table by moving this conversation to the living room."

We followed him without question, each of us thinking over what Kurt had said.

I knew how Madelyn coveted that artifact, so I wasn't too surprised when she said, "Very well, Kurt. I'll accept your suggestion. Benita, Andrea, and I will conduct a search in my bedroom. I trust the two of you to conduct your own personal search with the same honesty."

"Of course," Kurt said, looking puzzled that there could be any doubt.

We went upstairs, and through a few miserable moments of embarrassment, although the search was cursory. With the hot summer weather, neither Benita, Madelyn, nor I had enough on to hide the topaz.

So we filed downstairs and reported to Kurt and Aldo, who, naturally, hadn't found the topaz either.

"I am completely befuddled," Benita announced, which shouldn't have been news to anyone.

Kurt's forehead kept wrinkling and smoothing, wrinkling and smoothing, as a signal that he was trying to think things out. Finally he asked, "Any ideas?"

"Yes," Madelyn said. "Let's forget all about the artifact for now and play cards." I could see that she was making an attempt to keep strong and steady, but there were deep lines and shadows around her eyes, and her fingers trembled.

Fortunately, a deck was found in the drawer of one of the end tables. I wondered if I should inform her that my knowledge of bridge was scanty. I didn't have to worry about it. After one hand she knew, so I sat out and Aldo sat in. It was also obvious that if my bridge game was bad, Aldo's was worse. We tried a couple of other games, even my wild suggestion of crazy eights, but gave up in exasperation.

Madelyn slammed the deck down on the table. "This is ridiculous!" she stated. "I should have let my instincts guide me and refused to come on this dreadful trip."

I kept quiet, not wanting to add to her problems by reminding her that it was *my* instincts, not hers, that she had ignored.

"In the first place," she went on, "Justin was being just too, too secretive, and I don't appreciate being made to play his games. Why he wanted to include Norton I don't know, unless it was just plain greed. It's common knowledge that Franklin Granakee has had some dealings with people on the other side of the law. He certainly wasn't particular where his fortune came from."

"Come now," Benita said. She drummed her fingertips on the table, and her voice was tight. "I just can't believe that."

"I've heard it from more than one source."

"Gossip just doesn't become you, Madelyn."

Madelyn looked surprised. "It's not gossip. We need to share any knowledge we have."

Benita put her hands to her head. "I don't want to talk about Norton. I keep remembering—"

But Madelyn wouldn't give up. "Do you suppose that Justin knew Norton's real identity? Remember his saying something about one of us sailing under false colors?"

I immediately thought about Kurt. Maybe he was the one the judge was referring to, thinking of Kurt's double identity as a huge joke.

Then Madelyn surprised me by saying, "It's also possible, Benita, that Justin could have been referring to you. Who were you representing on the side? That dealer in Los Angeles perhaps?"

Benita tried to look surprised and wounded, but it didn't work. She leaned back in her chair and sighed. "No, it wasn't Ableman's, if that's who you're referring to. I'm not at liberty to divulge my client's name. You can respect that, can't you?"

"Did Justin think you were representing the gallery?"

"I hope so." Her eyes suddenly became swarmy with tears, and she said, "You know as well as I do, Madelyn, that everything can't be open and aboveboard in our business. I had a chance to make a huge commission, and I went for it, because I badly needed it. And then the way it turned out—nothing but bad luck." She mopped at her eyes and went on. "I'm on a roll of bad luck. Two marriages gone sour, my new car repossessed, a lost commission . . ."

"Sorry," Madelyn said, but she didn't sound sorry. "Knowing you, Benita, I'm sure that you were desperate enough to do anything to get possession of that artifact."

"Desperate. Yes, that's the word for it." She sighed, then abruptly realized what she had said and snapped, "Don't try to trick me, Madelyn! I had nothing to do with those deaths, and I don't know where in blazes that artifact is!"

Aldo yawned widely and stretched. "I'm going to bed," he said, and got to his feet.

"I'm tired too," Benita said. She fluttered upward and held out a hand to Madelyn. "I think we should all go up together."

"Are you still frightened?" I asked her.

She looked a little embarrassed. "I admit I was upset at first, but seen in this new light I—well, I'm angry instead of frightened. We've all been badly used."

"Especially the judge and Mr. Granakee," I mumbled.

Aunt Madelyn, who had come to my side, poked me as a signal to watch what I said, so I meekly followed the others up the stairs to bed. With the lights off the living room was a dark, cavernous hole, and I had to convince myself that the room was empty, that the noises I heard were the natural noises of night, and nothing was creeping up the stairs behind me.

Outside my door Madelyn stopped and put a hand on my arm. "I keep thinking about your mother," she said. "She'd be so upset with me for involving you in this situation." I was surprised to see tears in her eyes.

"Mom wouldn't blame you, Aunt Madelyn. How could you know what would happen?"

She didn't seem to hear me. "I remember when you were born," she murmured. "I was so excited that I cut class to stay at the hospital until your father came rushing out with the good news. You were a very special baby." She smiled. "I guess I thought of you as so special because you've always been a carbon copy of your mother, and she—well, she was a wonderful big sister."

Madelyn blinked a couple of times, as though coming back to the present, and I could almost see her backbone stiffen. "We'll get you home safely,

Andrea," she said firmly. "Don't doubt it for a minute."

She smiled, and I tried unsuccessfully to smile back. No matter how confident Madelyn sounded, I knew she was as frightened as I was.

From somewhere below us a tired board in the house popped, and I jumped and shuddered. Madelyn frowned in concern. "Would you like me to stay with you?"

I shook my head and tried to put her at ease. "I'm a big girl," I said. "I don't even need a night-light."

"Then I'll let you get your sleep," she answered. Gently she kissed my cheek. "Good night, Andrea."

"Good night, Aunt Madelyn," I murmured. Impulsively, I reached out and hugged her. "Thanks," I whispered.

I stood in the upper hall for a moment after Madelyn had gone into her room. The house creaked again, and I backed against the wall, trying to stare into the darkness. My imagination was ready to leap out of hand. I tried to hold it down, but it fought back, so I dashed into my bedroom. Groaning with relief, I locked the door.

The veranda doors were open wide, and moonlight from a clear sky poured into the room. Before I turned on the light I moved to close the doors, but suddenly someone stepped out of the bathroom, quickly slipped behind me, and clapped a hand over my mouth.

"Don't make a sound!" he whispered.

CHAPTER

~~~~~~~~~~~~~~~~~~~~~~

11

I struggled and tried unsuccessfully to make shouting noises in the back of my throat until the voice whispered, "I knew you'd do that! Will you just shut up!"

Relief turned my legs to wet spaghetti, and I collapsed against Pete, managing to throw him off balance, so we ended up in a heap on the floor.

"You're heavier than you look," he muttered as he tugged one of his legs out from under me.

"Thanks," I grumbled sarcastically.

"Hey, it doesn't bother me. Nobody's perfect."

"You really scared me, Pete! My heart's still banging away!"

"Really? Let's see."

I pushed him away. "What are you doing here?"

"Taking care of you. What else?"

"Wait a minute." I realized that even our whispers could probably be heard through the open veranda doors, so I jumped up and closed them tightly, then groped my way back to where I'd left

Pete sitting on the floor, his back against the wall. "Did you get a chance to go aboard the power-boat?" I asked.

"Yeah, I did. I looked over every inch of that boat, and the PI hadn't come back by the time I left it."

"He's here at the house," I said. "Tell me. What do you think about the boat?"

"It's a neat boat. It's got this terrific computer navigational device that—"

"Don't get sidetracked. I don't know what you're talking about anyway. What I want to know is, will we be able to use the boat?"

"I know how to operate it. No problem."

I shifted to snuggle against him, and he put an arm around me. "Thank you, Pete."

"For what?"

"For being such a good person. I trusted you, and I was right. You could have taken that boat and left the island, but you didn't. You stayed."

"Do you think I would leave you with a murderer?" Pete's breath was warm against my hair, and his other arm went around me. "You don't need to thank me for being brave, for putting aside everything else in order to be with you. You're very special, Andy. You—"

I would have let Pete go on, but a floorboard on the veranda cracked, and I quickly put a finger over his lips. "Someone's out there," I whispered.

I could feel Pete tense. We waited, ears straining to catch another sound.

It came. Another board creaking under some-one's weight, but farther down the veranda now,

away from my room. And another step, even farther away. I shivered with relief, or maybe it was
Pete who shivered. We were so close together it
was hard to tell the difference.

"In case we need to take the boat then, we're
ready," I said. "You've got everything you need."

"Except the ignition key," he said.

I pulled away and stared at him, barely able to
see him, even though my eyes had adjusted to the
dark. I was so angry, it was probably just as well he
couldn't see my face. "The brave hero!" I said.
"You chose to stay and protect me! Ha! You
couldn't take the boat out, because you didn't find
the key."

"That was just one minor reason," he said.

"Darn!" I said. I leaned back against the wall,
my arms folded tightly.

"Hey, Andy, look at it this way. I'm here, aren't
I? I could have gone back to my own boat."

"Just why are you here? I want an honest answer."

"Because you're here, and I really do want to
help you."

The anger began to dissipate, taking with it the
hot tension from my head and neck and shoulders.
I unfolded my arms and began to relax. "You don't
have to be here, you know."

"Why don't you just go to bed?" he asked. "I'll
sit here on the floor and keep watch."

"You'll get stiff. You'll be uncomfortable."

"All in the line of duty. You don't need to thank
me . . ." he began, but I giggled and sidled closer.

"I can't sleep," I said. "I'll sit here with you.

Maybe if we go over everything that has happened, we can come closer to figuring out who might have killed the judge and Mr. Granakee."

So, one by one, we talked about everyone who had come to the island, even including Aunt Madelyn. We didn't leave Ellison out either. And we came up with nothing, except for that strange prickly feeling that poked at the back of my mind and refused to turn itself into words I could see and understand. What was I missing? What was I trying to remember?

I thought about it so hard that it surprised me when the idea began to fall into place. "Pete," I murmured, and discovered that I was lying on the floor, a pillow under my head. The room was dark, still touched with moonlight from the open veranda doors, and I had no idea what time it was.

"Pete?" I sat up, trying to rub away the furry taste and feel of sleep as I reached for him, looked for him. But Pete wasn't there.

I stumbled to my feet, wildly scanning the room, and discovered a mound in the middle of my bed. I ripped back the blanket, and the mound mumbled something.

"Pete!" I hissed. "What are you doing in my bed?"

He groaned and struggled up on his elbows, shook his head to clear it, and said, "Well, you weren't using it."

"I thought you were going to keep watch."

"It's your turn." He dropped down again and groped for the blanket.

"No!" I pulled the blanket away from his reach

and shook his shoulders. "Listen to me, Pete. You've got to wake up. I think I know who committed the murders!"

This got his attention. His eyes opened wide, and he sat up, swinging his legs over the edge of the bed. "Who?" he asked.

"Aldo."

Pete looked so puzzled that I hurried to explain. "The judge said someone was sailing under false colors. He said this when I said that people were not always what they seemed to be."

"He could have been talking about his private investigator-secretary, having a good laugh about it."

"I thought so at one time, but I don't think so now. Let me finish what I have to say. I think that the judge was talking about people themselves, not the clients they claimed to represent. So he couldn't have been referring to Benita."

"What about Aldo's client?"

"It's not *who* he is, it's *what* he is."

"I know I'm awake, but I can't seem to follow you. Are you making this more complicated than it's supposed to be?"

"No, no! Listen!" I was so eager to explain that I grabbed Pete by the shoulders. "That wasn't all that the judge said. When he met Aldo for the first time, on the dock in Fort Lauderdale, he said that he looked familiar. He told Aldo that he had a good memory and sooner or later he'd remember where he'd met him."

"That's not much of a reason for killing him."

"Aldo must have thought so. I don't think he

counted on the judge having any idea who he really was. Maybe he and the judge had never met. It could be that the judge had only seen Aldo's picture—maybe in a newspaper."

I stopped for breath. "And then there's Franklin Granakee. Aunt Madelyn mentioned that Mr. Granakee had been involved with people on the other side of the law. Mr. Granakee said he knew everyone who had come to bid for the artifact. I didn't think anything about it at the time, but he had to have been including Aldo."

"You think he knew him?"

"Knew him or knew about him. Look, Pete, maybe Aldo wasn't representing anyone. Maybe he had come just to steal the artifact. Aldo might have been afraid that if the judge remembered him, he'd have no chance to get possession of the artifact. And later he either realized that Mr. Granakee would tell the others about him or maybe Mr. Granakee even threatened to do so. Aldo's the one who'd have a reason to kill Judge Arlington-Hughes and Mr. Granakee. Don't you agree?"

Pete thought hard for a few minutes. "Maybe you're right," he said.

"So what can we do next?"

"I'm darned sure not going to wake up Aldo and ask him if he's the murderer!"

"Be serious."

"I get too scared when I'm serious."

I plopped onto the bed next to Pete. "I told Kurt I'd let him know if I uncovered anything. I think now is the time to tell him what we know."

"Not 'know.' What we *suspect.*"

"We need to get Kurt's help, Pete."

"Do we have to? I told you, I don't trust that guy."

"Can you handle Aldo yourself?"

Pete sighed and stood up. "Okay. Where do we find Kurt?"

"Probably in his room."

Pete walked to the doors, opened them, and stared up at the sky. "Can't we wait until it's light? If we knock on his door in the dark, everyone in the house will pop out into the hall to see what's going on. They're all jumpy." He walked back to where I was sitting. "As a matter of fact, we're taking a big chance doing so much talking here. Even though we've been whispering, someone might have heard us."

I climbed off the bed. "Then let's go downstairs and talk, or outside. That's even better. I can't go back to sleep."

A meager sift of moonlight kept us from blindly stumbling on our way down the hall and stairs. We moved slowly, clutching each other, trying to make as little noise as possible. Pete breathed through his mouth in short, erratic gasps. I tended to hold my breath with each creak of the wooden floor and stairs, letting it out in a whoosh when I couldn't hold it any longer. We sounded like two candidates for an oxygen tent. In a strange way it was comforting to me that Pete was as frightened as I was. This was something we were involved in together.

"So far, so good," Pete whispered.

I listened intently. No footsteps, no lights turned on, no one calling "Who's there?"

"I don't think anyone heard us," I whispered back, relief so strong that my legs felt wobbly.

"Which way now? Back door? Front door?"

"They wouldn't hear the back door as easily as they would the front door. But Ellison's room is somewhere downstairs and close by, so we'll still have to be as quiet as possible."

Pete took my hand and began to lead me into the living room. But I balked and said, "You act as though you know the way."

For a moment there was complete silence. Then Pete whispered, "I got a pretty good idea of the layout of the house before you all went upstairs to bed. I found your room without any trouble. Remember?"

His face was so close to mine that as I nodded agreement my cheek rubbed against his, and I breathed in his warm, salty, sunburned smell, which was even more comforting than his words had been. "I'm sorry I was suspicious, Pete. I guess it's because I'm so frightened."

"We need each other, Andy," Pete said.

I nodded again. This time our lips brushed together for just a second, and Pete said, "Let's sit on the sand in the moonlight."

What was the matter with me? Why had I been suspicious of Pete? Was I so terrified that I couldn't think straight? I gave a little nudge to his shoulder and moved forward. "Let's go."

The living room was darker than the hall, and

Pete immediately banged a foot into the leg of a table. "Ouch!" he said.

"Be quiet," I cautioned.

"Can't we use flashlights? They're on that table in the entry hall."

"I don't think we should. Someone might see the light."

"If they're all asleep, they won't. Stay here. I'll be right back." In a couple of minutes he returned with two flashlights and put one of them into my hands.

"Don't turn them on until we get outside. How do we know they're all asleep?"

Pete muttered something under his breath about wishing he'd gone to Mexico instead and moved forward, cautiously groping ahead before taking each step. I glanced around the room, trying to squint through the shadows, my imagination creeping ahead of me. A patch of darkness, too deep to penetrate, lay on the floor behind the table where the judge's body had lain. And in that high-backed chair—was someone sitting there? Was that the roundness of a head? The hiss of suddenly suppressed breathing? I squeezed even closer to Pete and managed to fight down the panic that threatened to burst through me like hot fireworks.

Making our way through the room was slow work, but eventually we crossed the living room and dining room and entered the kitchen, where the open windows allowed moonlight to spill in without interference. We arrived at the back door as quickly as though it were home base and we'd been in a race.

"I'm not too happy about all this," Pete said. He moved close to me and put a hand on my arm as I reached out to open the back door. "Just do me one favor."

"Sure," I said. "What is it?"

"When you talk to Kurt, tell him whatever you like about your suspicions, but don't tell him you know where the artifact is."

"I don't think you need to worry," I said. "We've figured out that the murderer is Aldo. That means that Kurt is in the clear."

"I don't trust him."

"That's just because you don't like him."

"You wouldn't like him either if he'd kicked your butt out of town. Come on, Andy. Promise. I know you keep your promises. See—I trust *you*."

"Okay," I told him. "Nothing about the artifact." Again I reached for the doorknob. Again Pete stopped me.

"One more thing," he said. "When we find him you talk to him alone. Don't tell him about me. Don't tell him I'm here on the island."

"Pete?"

"And don't stand around asking stupid questions. Let's go."

As I opened the door Pete stepped aside, motioning me to go ahead. I practically ran down the half dozen or so back steps to the grass and held up my flashlight, fumbling for the switch.

"Should I turn this on now?" I whispered.

"Why not?" A shape quickly separated itself

from the shadows at the side of the house, and
before I realized what was happening a beam of
light shone directly into my face.

I held up an arm to shield my eyes. "Stop that!" I
cried out. "What are you doing?"

The light was lowered, and the voice said,
"You're the one who should answer that question.
What are you doing out here by yourself at this
time of night?"

"Kurt?" I was so thankful to recognize his voice
that it took me a moment to realize what he had
asked. Here by myself?

I whirled around to look behind me. The
kitchen door was closed snugly, and there was no
sign of Pete.

CHAPTER

~~~~~~~~~~~~~~

12

"Andrea?" Kurt sounded puzzled. "Answer my question."

I turned to face him. "I came outside to look for you."

"Why?"

"You told me to tell you if I discovered anything important, and I have."

"What did you find out?" He waited, and while I was trying to think of what to do next, he added, "Would you rather get away from the house before you tell me? Maybe that's a good idea."

"No!" I glanced over my shoulder at the house, which was so quiet it seemed deserted. Pete must still be in the kitchen. He must have seen Kurt, or maybe he suspected that he was out here and sent me out alone to find out. I didn't want to get too far away from Pete.

"There's no need for you to be afraid," Kurt said. "Walk down to the dock with me. We can talk there."

As I hesitated again he switched off his flashlight and said, "We don't need flashlights. There's enough moonlight so that we can see where we're going. We can pick up the path over there."

I didn't have a choice. Whatever his reason, Pete had told me not to let Kurt know that he was on the island, and he trusted me to keep his presence secret. So I walked with Kurt over the lawn to the path and down the path to the dock. We walked almost to the end of the dock before Kurt sat down on the edge, his legs dangling over the water. I sat next to him.

The sea wasn't beautiful now. The moon had dropped low enough in the sky to have sucked its silver reflection from the surface of the water, leaving in its place a deep, menacing blackness that surged around the dock. I imagined the large sea creatures—the knife-tailed manta rays, the deadly barracuda, and the sharks who never sleep —just under the surface of the water, watching and waiting. I pulled my feet in close to my body and hugged my knees before I spoke.

"I know who committed the murders," I said. "Aldo."

Kurt was silent. He watched me, studied me. Finally he said, "Is that it? You must have a reason for what you said."

"I do." I hoped it would sound as sensible as when Pete and I figured it out a little while ago.

"What are you waiting for? Let's hear it."

I took a deep breath and jumped in. "Okay. In the first place, I don't think that Aldo is representing some sheik in the Mideast. I think he's a professional art thief."

"Then he could have just helped himself to the artifact by force, left the island, and saved a lot of time and trouble. Right?"

"No! That's not right. I think he's the kind of thief who'd work with his wits and skill and avoid force as much as possible." He frowned, and I added quickly, "The point is that none of the people who came to bid on the topaz knew that the others would be here. Aldo thought he was coming to deal with the judge and that would be that."

"Go on," he said as I paused. His voice was so low, I could barely hear it.

"When Aldo realized what the situation was, he went along with it. I don't know what he had in mind. Maybe he was thinking up ways to steal the artifact from whoever bid for it and got it, but a couple of things went wrong for him. The judge told him that he looked familiar, and sooner or later he'd remember where he'd seen him. When Judge Arlington-Hughes referred to someone present sailing under false colors, Aldo thought the judge had figured it out."

Kurt shook his head. "You didn't know the judge," he said. "He liked a good private joke, even if it wasn't very funny to anyone except himself. He was getting a big kick out of passing me off as his secretary, when he'd hired me as a private investigator and bodyguard."

"You were his bodyguard too?"

He groaned at the surprise in my voice and said,

"Don't say it. Don't think I don't keep reminding myself that I let him down."

"I'm sorry. I—"

His voice was brusque. "If you've got any more to tell me, get on with it."

"Okay, to get back to what the judge said. I think that Aldo couldn't take the chance that the judge had figured out who he was, so Aldo decided to simply kill the judge and steal the artifact. He hoped there'd be no problem with the murder, that everyone would accept it as an accidental death."

I paused, but Kurt didn't say anything. He was listening to me so intently, it gave me more confidence. I went on. "Franklin Granakee told us, when he came aboard the boat, that he knew everyone, and Aunt Madelyn said later that it was a known fact that Mr. Granakee had dealings with art thieves. It's possible that Mr. Granakee threatened to tell the police about Aldo. So—don't you see—Aldo had to kill him too."

I waited tensely. I was so sure of what I'd told him. What would I do if he said that my idea was stupid, or—like Mom sometimes said—that my imagination had run away with me again?

Kurt seemed to think for a long time. Finally he said, "You could be right."

I sighed loudly, thankfully. "Then you can arrest him!"

"It's not that easy."

"Why not? You have a gun."

He stared at me sharply. "What makes you think that?"

I gulped. "Oh. Well, because you're a private investigator. Don't all private investigators carry guns?"

"You watch too much television," he grumbled.

Relief at not having given Pete away made me reckless. "If you don't carry a gun, then how do you make an arrest?"

"As a licensed investigator I don't make arrests. I get information for my clients. If I uncover criminal activity, I inform the police, and they make the arrests."

"Then what will we do about Aldo? He's a murderer. Can't we lock him in one of the rooms so he can't hurt anyone else?"

"We'll leave him alone," Kurt said.

"Just because you can't arrest him doesn't mean that—"

He interrupted. "That's not the reason. The reason is that we still don't know the location of the artifact."

"Do you think Aldo has it?"

"Who knows? If he has it, and he's free, he could lead us to it."

"If you knew where the artifact was, would you do something about Aldo?"

"Yes. If I had that topaz in hand, I'd do anything you'd ask me to do."

It's time that someone else knew, I thought. *I'm tired of handling this by myself. Kurt was the investigator. He'd be the logical one to tell.*

The moon had disappeared, and I realized that we were seated in a gray haze from which outlines were beginning to emerge. Kurt's face grew real and vivid, the muscles around his eyes and neck strained and tense. His voice was raspy and low, and it frightened me. "Do you know where the artifact is, Andrea?"

My fingers were twisted together so tightly that they hurt. I had promised Pete I wouldn't tell Kurt. I had to keep my promise. I looked directly into Kurt's eyes and said, "We've all been searching. It hasn't shown up yet."

"Keep looking," he said, and smiled. The patronizing tone was back. "Maybe we could have a bonus, a nice cash award for the person who finds it."

From where I sat I could see through the now-clear, pale water to the waving tendrils and spines of sea grasses and poisonous animals. My backbone felt as though those wet, clammy, deadly fingers were trailing down it, and I involuntarily shivered. Was Kurt just putting out feelers? Or had I gone too far, and did he now suspect me?

He stood up, and I scrambled to my feet, wishing I had Pete here to hang on to. "I'm going back to the house," he said.

"What should I do?"

He put a hand on my shoulder. His fingers pressed a little too tightly, and I winced. "Keep looking. We've got to find that artifact before the boat comes back this afternoon. Understand?"

"Yes."

I tried to wiggle out from under his grip, teetering at the edge of the dock, but he didn't release me until after he said, "If you find the topaz or discover who has it, come to me. To no one else but me. Until the police arrive, I'm in charge of this investigation."

As Kurt strode briskly off the dock, I stumbled forward and caught my balance. By the time I looked up he had disappeared. What was the matter with me? Couldn't I trust anyone? Kurt was the closest to police authority that we had on the island, and he was right. The artifact belonged in his care. I should get it now—right now!—so Kurt could lock up Aldo and the whole matter would be settled. And once the artifact was in the hands of the police, I could explain about the Peruvian government and— Would the police pay any more attention to me than to anyone else? Would they let me give it to the Peruvian consul or ambassador?

I'd made a promise to Pete, so before doing anything I'd have to check with him. All I had to do was find him.

The sky was a clear, silvery blue, and colors were changing from pastels to brights. Ellison was probably up and making breakfast, so surely Pete wouldn't still be in the kitchen. He had probably slipped out of the back door soon after Kurt and I walked down to the dock. Had he gone back to his boat? Or would he still be around? I sighed as I thought about trekking once more down the beach and across the island.

I hadn't gone far when I felt his presence again. "Okay," I said, "where are you?"

"Shhhh!" he hissed at me from the trees. "You're too close to the house. Anyone who came out on the front porch could see you. Keep going. Walk a little farther."

I did, following the beach on its wide sweep inland. As soon as I was out of sight of the house, Pete burst through the bushes to join me.

"What happened? Didn't he believe you about Aldo?"

"I'm pretty sure he did," I said.

"Then why didn't he do something? Arrest him? Tie him up? Lock him in a closet? Whatever?"

"Because the artifact hasn't been found yet. For all Kurt knows, Aldo is in possession of it."

Pete's sunburned nose crinkled in the middle as he thought. "That's good, I guess. Yes, that's definitely good, because he doesn't suspect you of having the artifact."

"I think I should give it to him."

"What!"

"That is, depending on if you know the answer to my question."

Pete's voice was edgy. "What kind of a game are we playing?"

"It's not a game. It's a very important question." I sat on the sand, which was already becoming warm from the sun, and Pete dropped down beside me. "Your father is an attorney, so I'm hoping you might know the answer to this from hearing things he's said. If the artifact is turned over to the police, what would they do with it?"

He didn't hesitate for a minute. "Hold it for evidence until the murder investigation is over and the case comes to trial," he said, "which could be for a period of a number of months to a number of years, depending on continuances, scheduling, all that stuff. And then we've got something else to consider. What police are we talking about? We aren't in U.S. jurisdiction here. So we could add extradition, and who knows how long that would take? Also, somewhere along the line that artifact could prove to be too much of a temptation."

I shivered. "I'm glad you explained all that. I had almost decided to give the artifact to Kurt."

Pete gave a sharp intake of breath. "You told him that you had taken it?"

"No! I didn't, because I promised you I wouldn't, and I keep my promises."

He smiled and put an arm around my shoulders. "Yeah," he said. "You really do. So he doesn't know about the artifact, and he doesn't know about me."

I doodled in the sand with one finger. "It might be safer for you if he did know about you."

"It might be safer for you if he doesn't."

I looked up at him. "What does that mean?"

"I keep remembering what a mean jerk he is. I remember his big foot. You've started thinking of him as an upholder of law and order. One of us is wrong."

"So? What do we do next?"

Pete bent to kiss me. "I think it's time to meet the family," he said.

I giggled. "Be serious."

"I am serious," he said. "I want to meet your Aunt Madelyn."

"And ask her for my hand?"

"You're a weird girl. What would I do with your hand? I've got two of my own."

I pushed away from him and said, "What nonsense are you talking about?"

"It may be necessary to leave this island in a hurry," Pete said. "If so, we don't want to scare the pants off your aunt. Therefore, we meet ahead of time, nice and friendly like, and let her get used to me."

"You don't know my Aunt Madelyn. She'd never get used to someone like you."

"Is she a tyrant? A monster? A tough customer?"

"No. I used to think so, because she's—well, she's my mother's sister, but she's not warm and outgoing like Mom. Madelyn's dedicated to her job, and I didn't understand her for a long time until I realized that she really is lonely." I turned to Pete, adding, "I wonder if people can be so lonely that they forget how to love."

"Oh, tell me about it," Pete moaned, and made a grab for me, but I was quicker than he was and jumped to my feet.

"When do you want to meet Aunt Madelyn?" I held out a hand to help him up.

"As soon as you can set it up. Just give me time to get back to the boat for a few things, like breakfast. When you want me walk out on the downstairs veranda. I'll be watching."

"So will Kurt. You may run into him."

"Not if I'm sharper and faster than he is. For a PI, he doesn't move very quietly. He clomps through the woods like a two-hundred-and-forty-pound elephant. Did you see that movie last year about the mummy with the hacksaw who—"

"No mummies. I couldn't take it. I'll see you

later." I turned and ran back to the house. Pete was crazy. He was fun. He wasn't anything like Rick. Pete could even make me temporarily forget that there was so much here to be afraid of.

Madelyn was on the lower veranda and waved to me. As I ran up the steps she said, "I was looking for you. You haven't had breakfast yet."

"What about the others? It's still early. Didn't they sleep late?"

"Sleep? Who can sleep?" In spite of her makeup, which she'd carefully applied this morning, Madelyn looked tired and old.

"I'm sorry," I said, and gave her a hug.

She hugged me back.

"There's someone I want you to meet," I told her.

"Of course," she answered. "As soon as we get back to Palm Beach."

"Not in Palm Beach," I began, but Aldo stepped onto the veranda.

"If you've had breakfast, we can begin," he said.

I moved away from Madelyn. I hoped he hadn't heard what I'd said. My heart began to thump so loudly, I was afraid he could hear it. It was hard to meet his gaze, suspecting what I did about him. Making my expression as bland as possible, I asked, "Begin what?"

"A reenactment of the showing," he said.

"Showing?"

"Showing the artifact," Madelyn explained. "Remember—when Justin brought it out and displayed it to us."

"Kurt thought if we went over it again, one of us

might recall something important," Aldo added, "something related to the disappearance of the topaz."

I didn't like that idea at all. I tried to stall. "Could it wait until I've had breakfast?"

"It's a continental breakfast," Aldo said. "It won't take long."

"I hate to eat fast. It's not good for the digestion."

"I'll keep you company," he said, and it made me mad, because he might just as well have said "I'll make sure that you don't dawdle."

"We'll *all* keep you company," Aunt Madelyn said. "Benita's already in the dining room working on a caffeine jag, and Kurt is in the living room attempting to recreate the setting. We'll invite him to join us."

The only choice was to accept.

I drank a cup of coffee—hot this time—and munched through two large cinnamon rolls. I hated having four pairs of eyes on me while I ate. It made me so self-conscious that I couldn't pick the raisins out of the rolls. I've always hated raisins.

I hated being here. I hated the horrible things that had happened. I hated being pressured by these people who thought it was perfectly all right to steal a Peruvian artifact in the name of art. At the moment I was in such a bad mood that I didn't even feel too kindly toward the country of Peru.

"Have you finished your meal?" Aldo asked, and it didn't come out like a question.

"Yes." I laid my napkin on the table. They began

to rise, but I said, "Wait a minute! There's something else we should figure out first."

Each of them sat back down again and stared at me. "What?" Madelyn asked.

"We need to know who had access to the living room, who might have had time to strip that cord."

Aldo shrugged. "If the cord was deliberately stripped and not worn, it would take only a minute or two."

Madelyn spread out her hands and looked puzzled. "And all of us were in the living room, in and out, ever since we arrived."

"But who was in the living room alone after the stage was set for showing the jewel?"

Benita gaped at me. "We were together, examining the setting."

"Did anyone notice whether the lamp had been plugged in or what the cord looked like?"

Benita said nastily, "We had only candlelight to see by. You should remember that, since you were responsible for knocking out the generator."

Madelyn quickly said, "And then we were asked to go to the veranda for cocktails. Soon afterward Ellison called us, and we all went into the dining room for dinner."

"All of us?"

"Of course," Benita said.

"No," Madelyn said slowly. "As I remember, Aldo said he had a headache. He went upstairs to get some aspirin."

"That's correct," Aldo said. "I joined you later."

"I remember when you came into the dining

room." My hands were clammy as I spoke out, but I had started this line of thinking and it was important. "You would have had plenty of time to strip that lamp cord."

"I suppose so," he said, "but so would Madelyn and Benita. As you remember, Benita left because she was coughing, and Madelyn followed to make sure that Benita was all right."

"You did?" Benita asked, staring at Madelyn with wide eyes. "Then where were you? I went straight to my room, but I didn't see you."

Except for a slight twitch of her chin, Madelyn didn't lose her cool demeanor. "I went to your room. You weren't there."

"I was— Oh," Benita said. "That's right. I didn't go to my room. I went out on the lower veranda."

Madelyn shrugged both her eyebrows. Benita mumbled, "Well, I did. I did."

Aldo said to Kurt, "How about you? Did you leave the room?"

"I was right there the whole time," Kurt said.

I tried hard to think. "Wait a minute. Kurt was sitting next to me, and he did leave the dining room a number of times because he was taking Ellison's place in serving while Ellison worked on the generator."

"So there we are," Madelyn said. "We all had access to the living room. So did Ellison."

Ellison opened the door to the kitchen. "Somebody want me?" he asked.

"No," Benita said.

But Kurt said, "Yes, we do." He stood. "We're

going to reenact the showing of the artifact, and I'd like you to be present."

"I wasn't there," Ellison said.

"I know. But we need someone to sit in for Judge Arlington-Hughes."

Ellison took a step backward and cleared his throat twice before he could speak. "I—I don't like that. The judge is dead. We should let him be."

I stood up too. "Don't make him. Nobody would want to play that part."

"It's necessary," Kurt said.

The others followed him to the living room. Ellison and I dragged along behind them, both of us wishing we were somewhere else.

Just inside the door, Kurt turned to face us. "Here," he said, "on this table were candles in candle holders. I've tried to arrange the table as it was. If you can remember which candlestick you were holding, please pick it up. Since we've got daylight, we don't need to light the candles."

All of us hesitated, examining the candlesticks. How could we possibly remember? But suddenly I saw the small brass candle holder, and I remembered very clearly. Is this how the reenactment would work? In repeating our actions would someone remember that I reached out for the artifact? Trying hard not to visibly tremble, I squeezed in behind the others, who were grouping themselves around the table.

Ellison was led to the chair positioned behind the table, which had been neatly spread with the black velvet cloth. His eyes were wide with fright.

Kurt leaned against the wall near us, his gaze intent. He wasn't going to miss a thing.

I moved to the right of where I had been, standing next to Benita, but she gave me a little push. "No, no," she said. "You weren't standing there, Andrea. Aldo was. Aldo was on my right, and Norton was on his right, a little past the end of the table."

"Where he could have seen the lamp cord," I said, trying to distract them.

I stepped to Madelyn's left, but Madelyn firmly moved me. "You stood next to Benita," she said. "You were between us."

She was correct, of course. I wished their memories weren't so good.

Aldo gave Ellison the small jewel box. "The judge took this from his pocket, opened it, and laid it on the table in front of us," he said. As Ellison clutched the box without moving, Aldo said firmly, "Open it, Ellison. Put it on the table, facing us."

With shaking hands Ellison held out the closed box. His fingers fumbled with the catch. In the silence I could hear my heart pounding in my ears.

With a sudden snap the box lid sprang back. Each of us let out a rush of breath as we stared at the empty box. It was like waiting for a ghost that didn't materialize, wondering if in some magic way the topaz would still lie there, glittering under the monkey's tiny golden paws, as it did on Friday night.

"It was the most beautiful stone I've ever seen." Madelyn's voice was low, as though she were speaking only to herself. "It had such depth, such clarity, and it glowed in the candlelight."

"But Justin told us to blow out the candles," Benita said. "And we did, except for Andrea."

Aldo picked up the story. "The judge turned the switch on the lamp, but nothing happened."

"He blamed Kurt, who was supposed to have plugged in the lamp," Madelyn said.

I tried to swallow. My throat was so dry it hurt, and the black velvet wavered and rippled and seemed to rise in a smothering haze.

Aldo said, "The judge reached down to plug in the lamp. Then Andrea's candle—"

"Don't ask me to do that!" Ellison clutched the edge of the table, his eyes rimmed with white. He looked sick.

"Someone pushed me!" I murmured. "The candle fell out of my hand and went out."

"Everyone was pushing forward," Madelyn said, "and Benita—"

Benita gasped, one hand over her forehead. "Wait! I remember something!" She slowly turned toward her left, toward Madelyn and me. "What did I see? Was it an arm reaching out? Yes. Yes, I saw an arm!"

"Whose arm?" Aldo whispered.

Lips parted, as though she were in a trance, Benita stared into space, trying to grasp the memory. I couldn't let this continue or she was going to remember! "No!" I screamed. "Stop it!" And I flung my candlestick to the floor.

CHAPTER

~~~~~~~~~~~~~~~~~~~~~~~~~~~

13

Benita screeched, and her candlestick went flying as she clapped her hands over her ears. This was too much for Ellison. He jumped to his feet so quickly that the table flew over, banging him in the shins. Without waiting to hear what Kurt would say, he hobbled from the room, looking like a sand crab scrambling sideways toward the safety of the sea.

I wrapped my arms around Aunt Madelyn. My scream may have been an act, but there was no pretense in the fear that lay like a wrapping of ice under my skin. She tried to soothe me, and I was awfully glad to have her there to hang on to.

Kurt picked up the table and slammed it back into place with such force that Benita opened her eyes and lowered her hands. Leaning on the table, his arms rigid, he glared at her and demanded, "Go on! You saw an arm. Whose arm?"

"Don't yell at me!" Benita began to cry. "I've

cooperated all along, and what happened wasn't my fault! I tried! But I don't know what I saw!"

"Okay, okay," Aldo said. "Calm down and think. You said that you saw an arm reach out."

"I know I said that, but I'm not sure. I saw a movement. It may have been something else. You've got me so confused. Ellison is right. We shouldn't have done this."

Kurt turned his attention to me. "Why did you scream?"

"Because I was frightened!" My voice trembled as I answered. "The way Benita was talking was like—well, like the way someone talks who is holding a séance and communicating with the dead."

Madelyn leaned back to look at me sharply. "When did you ever go to a séance?"

"I didn't, but I've seen them in movies."

Aldo, who was obviously making a deliberate effort to get himself under control, tried to speak calmly. "Perhaps we should try this again."

"No!" Benita, Madelyn, and I spoke together.

"Besides," Madelyn added, "you'll never get Ellison to cooperate after what happened."

"I want to lie down," Benita said.

"How about sitting out on the veranda?" I asked. "It's breezy and comfortable, and you can look at the sea."

"That's a good idea," Madelyn said. "Andrea and I will go with you." She didn't mention Aldo or Kurt. I wondered if they'd upset her, too, with this terrifying reenactment.

Neither Aldo nor Kurt said a word. They quietly watched us as we left the living room through the open, shuttered doors. I wasn't worried about what Aldo might do. Knowing that Kurt was in the house watching him made me feel a lot more secure.

We helped lower Benita onto a reclining lawn chair, where she plopped, her legs giving out. "I wish I had never gotten involved in this," she whimpered. "I want to go home."

"The boat will be here late this afternoon," Madelyn reassured her.

"That's hours away!" Benita complained. "Who knows what will happen between now and then?"

My thoughts exactly.

But Madelyn said firmly, "It's ridiculous to worry about what might happen. We'll simply rest here on the veranda and enjoy the breeze and the sunlight. You must admit that it's a beautiful day."

She and I chose chairs a little apart from Benita. Maybe it was the creaking rhythm of our rocking chairs, but Benita seemed to relax, and pretty soon her eyes closed.

"Do you think she's asleep?" I asked.

"I hope so!" Madelyn said. "She can be—umm—difficult to deal with."

"Sometimes she acts like a child."

"Unfortunately, she did not have a pretty childhood—foster homes, one in which she was abused."

"Aunt Madelyn," I said, "people are so complex. I mean, like Benita, and like Aldo. He frightens me, and yet he has a daughter my age, and his face lit up as he talked about her. And Kurt. I feel kind of sorry for him, because he was a popular jock in high school, and that was the only big moment in his life. But at the same time he's tough and mean —to Pete—uh—to some people—and he poses as the judge's secretary, only he's really a private investigator."

Madelyn sat upright. "He's what?"

I looked toward the house. No one seemed to be within earshot, but I didn't want to take the chance. "Walk with me down the beach," I said as I stood. "Come on, Aunt Madelyn. I'll explain."

She glanced over at Benita, who was breathing in a low, steady whistle. "I guess she won't miss us, but we'd better make it a short walk." She rose and put a hand on my arm. "Andrea, do you think I'm as complex as the others you've mentioned?"

I nodded.

"And how do you see me?"

"You're my aunt," I said. "I love you."

For a moment she looked as though she wasn't going to let me get away with an answer like that, but she smiled. "All right," she said. "Let's take that walk. I want to hear what you have to tell me."

We walked east, out of sight of the house, and I told her about Pete and what Pete had told me about Kurt. I knew that Pete was somewhere nearby because he had said he'd be.

Madelyn stopped, her toes digging into the damp sand. "This story is incredible, Andrea! You meet a strange boy on this island and actually trust him? Suppose he's the one who stole the artifact and killed Justin and Granakee?"

"I knew you'd think that," I said. "But he couldn't."

"Why not?"

I told her about my suspicions concerning Aldo. When I finished she said, "It does make sense." She shook her head impatiently. "But if that's the case, then Kurt obviously did not do the thorough job of investigating that Justin hired him to do, and because of his carelessness we have been put in this horrible situation. I'd like to tell him what I think of him!"

"No! You can't!" I said.

She waved my concern aside. "Well, of course I won't, but one point bothers me. Why is Aldo searching so intently for the artifact if he has it? Do you think he's putting on an act to deceive us?"

"No," I said. "He doesn't have the artifact."

She frowned as she thought. "I don't have it, and I really believe that Benita doesn't. But if Kurt has it, why would he have made us go through that horrible charade?"

"Kurt doesn't have it," I said.

She looked at me with wide eyes. "Andrea! Don't you realize? That Pete person is the only one left. He must have stolen the topaz!"

"He didn't, Aunt Madelyn. I took it."

She opened and shut her mouth a few times, but nothing came out. "I think Aldo planned to take it as soon as the lights went out," I said. "It just happened that I was closer to the topaz and beat him to it."

"Well," she said. "I never thought—" She broke off, still staring at me.

"None of them did," I said, "because I wasn't an invited guest. I just tagged along with you. I wasn't here to bid on the artifact, and besides, to them I'm just a kid, and kids don't count."

"But sooner or later someone will add things up," Madelyn said. "In fact, I wonder if Aldo has already begun to suspect you! What in the world should we do?"

"I think you should meet Pete," I said, and I turned toward the trees. "Pete, you're there, aren't you?"

He popped out from behind a tree and jumped to the sand.

Aunt Madelyn winced, but as I introduced them she graciously held out her right hand and behaved as though she were meeting Pete at an art gallery reception.

"I want you to trust me," Pete said.

"I have no reason to." Madelyn drew herself up like the cold, wicked queen again, withdrawing her hand.

Pete sighed. "I should have worn a tie, shouldn't I? I just didn't have one that goes with these shorts."

The tropical heat didn't make a dent in the chill Madelyn sent out. "I don't appreciate your attempts at humor," she told Pete. "They are totally out of place."

But Pete gave her a big smile. "We're all in a tight spot, and we need a little humor to keep from going bonkers. We also need each other, Aunt Madelyn."

"I am not *your* Aunt Madelyn."

His smile grew wider. "We'll make it only if you trust me. Hey, *I* trust *you.*"

"Please, Aunt Madelyn," I said.

"I don't sign blank checks," she said. "Suppose you tell me what you have in mind."

Pete looked at me. "I wish we could," he said, "but we haven't thought it all out yet."

"Young man," Madelyn said, "I have no idea what you're planning to do, or even who you are." She turned to me. "Do you have a good, solid reason for trusting this young man?"

"Yes," I said. "Pete makes me feel good about myself, and I haven't felt that way for a long time." Madelyn raised one questioning eyebrow, so I went on. "Everything seemed to be crashing in on me at once, Aunt Madelyn, and I felt like a little kid who wanted to hide until everything was back to the way it should be. I didn't want to admit that life keeps going forward, and situations change. I guess I didn't think I could handle my problems. But now I know that I can. I'm not a little kid, and whatever happens in my life—even whatever Mom and Dad decide to do with their lives—I'll be able to work it out. Now, do you understand?"

She didn't look convinced as she said, "You want me to trust this young man simply on the basis of your feelings about yourself? You haven't told me anything tangible about him."

I tried to think of something that would help. "Pete lives in Miami, Aunt Madelyn. Maybe you know his parents. His father is an attorney."

"Michaels?" A computer key clicked on in her

brain and she said to Pete, "Hamilton Michaels? Is he your father?"

"Yeah," Pete said.

Her features immediately softened. "Hamilton and Marion Michaels. They gave the Sartington Museum a generous loan of three fine Rembrandt sketches. Well. So, you're their son."

"Now will you trust him?" I asked.

"Perhaps," she said. "I admit I'm a little more inclined to do so."

"Pete," I said, "maybe we should tell her about—"

I didn't finish the sentence, because a panicky voice shouted down the beach, "Madelyn! Where are you?"

"It's Benita," I said. Pete ducked into the trees and I added to Madelyn, "Will you take her back to the house? Please? There's something I have to talk over with Pete."

Madelyn immediately turned and walked toward Benita. I heard them greet each other, then turn as though they were going toward the house. Their voices drifted away, and again the beach was silent.

"Come out. It's safe," I said to Pete.

He joined me on the sand. For a change, he was serious. "I think we're going to have to get off this island pretty quickly, Andy. The bad guys are going to start closing in."

I dropped cross-legged to the sand. Pete sat down beside me. "Aunt Madelyn said something about Kurt," I told him.

"She doesn't like him either?"

"Listen to me. It may be important. After I told her about Aldo she blamed Kurt for not doing the thorough job of investigating he was hired to do."

"That's important?"

Other things I remembered began to crowd into my mind. It was like opening a spigot. As the idea began to pour out it moved so quickly that it scared me. I took hold of Pete's hand. I needed to hang on to someone. "What if Kurt knew about Aldo's criminal affiliations? What if they worked this out together?"

Pete's eyes grew wide. "He'd be up to doing something like that."

"I remember that Madelyn, Benita, and Mr. Granakee were upset that others had been invited, but Aldo wasn't. What if he knew the others would be there, because Kurt had told him?"

"Do you think they planned to kill the judge?"

"I'm afraid so. Maybe Kurt stripped the covering from the wires on the cord. Maybe Aldo did. But once the judge was dead, they'd grab the artifact and leave the island. That's why the powerboat was hidden in the cove."

Pete nodded. "It's a pretty good guess."

"It's not a guess," I said. "I'm sure of it. Aldo was upset because he was going to miss his daughter's birthday party on Sunday afternoon. He told me he'd promised her he'd be there, so he knew he'd be leaving Friday night. If Aldo had been an innocent guest, enjoying the judge's weekend invitation, there was no way he could get to a birthday party in New Jersey on Sunday."

The rest of it spilled out. "When I told Kurt I was

suspicious that Aldo was mixed up with organized crime, he answered that if that were the case, Aldo could have just taken the artifact by force and left the island."

Pete whistled. "And to do that he'd have to know about the boat. Kurt really gave that one away."

I climbed to my feet. Pete got up, too, and said, "We've got to think fast. We're running out of time. What are we going to do?"

"There seems to be only one thing to do," I said. "I'm going to tell Kurt that I've got the artifact."

Pete groaned and kicked at a tree root that curled up and into the sand. "You're going to give it to Kurt? That's crazy! That's dumb!"

"Pete, listen to me." I put my hands on his shoulders and looked into his eyes. "I'm going to tell you where I put the artifact. I hid it in a cave west of the house," I said, and went on to give him a complete description of the limestone promontory and how to find it.

For a moment he was silent. Then "Thanks, Andy," he said. The words were so soft I could hardly hear them, but the crinkle lines deepened around his eyes. I reached out and hugged him.

Pete hugged back, enthusiastically, then suddenly broke away. "Okay," he said. "Let's go back to your plan A, B, or whatever."

"You mean my plan to tell Kurt I've got the artifact?"

"You can't. What do you think he'll do to you then?"

"He'll wait for me, because that's what I'll tell

him to do. I'll tell him that I've hidden the artifact, but I won't tell him where. And I'll tell him to wait for me in the living room. That will keep him out of the way and give you the chance to do what you have to do."

"Which is what?"

"Hot-wire the boat."

His eyes grew wide and his mouth fell open.

"You once hot-wired a car to start it," I said. "And you said a powerboat ran sort of like a car. So couldn't you do the same thing with the motorboat?"

He thought a minute. "Yeah," he said. "With a little luck I ought to be able to."

"Then bring it around to the promontory near the cave. Were my directions enough? Do you think you can find it?"

"I can find it."

"Watch the house, Pete. I'll send Aunt Madelyn and Benita and Eliison to meet you before I talk to Kurt. As soon as they reach the woods, take them to the boat."

"That would leave you alone with Kurt and Aldo," he said.

"Only for a couple of minutes." My hands were getting clammy again. I hoped Pete wouldn't see how frightened I was.

But maybe he did, because he frowned. "I ought to stick around."

"There won't be time."

"I wouldn't want anything bad to happen to you, Andy."

"It won't." My voice sounded a lot more positive

than I felt. We looked at each other without speaking for a moment. Then I said, "That's it. Are you ready?"

"Ready," he said.

I kissed him quickly, turned, and ran down the beach toward the house.

Madelyn and Benita were seated once again on the veranda. I motioned to Madelyn to join me, and she hurried down the steps. She wasn't the calm, collected person I was used to, and I hoped the others hadn't noticed her trembling hands.

I made a show of hugging her, wondering who might be watching, and whispered, "Where's Ellison?"

"In the kitchen."

"Where are Kurt and Aldo?"

"In the living room. After what you told me about Aldo, I'm so thankful that Kurt is here to keep an eye on him."

She had more to say, but I didn't let her. "Take Benita with you right now," I said. "Go around the house to the kitchen, get Ellison, and head straight toward the woods. Pete will take over then. Do what he tells you."

"I'll need more explanation than that," she said.

"No. That's it. There isn't time. You're going to have to trust Pete and me and cooperate, Aunt Madelyn. This may be the only chance we've got."

Her eyes narrowed as she thought, and I could almost see her thoughts whirling behind them. Finally she looked up at me. "Is there something else you're not telling me?"

"Yes," I said. "And we're talking about trust again."

She took a deep breath and with it seemed to grow taller and straighter. "Very well," she said. "I'll do as you say." She motioned to Benita, calling, "Come, dear. We must not sit and stagnate. We're off for a stroll."

Benita slowly joined her, grumbling about not wanting so much exercise, and I ran up the veranda steps and into the living room, where Kurt was slouched in an armchair, reading a magazine.

I looked around before I spoke. "Where's Aldo?"

"In his room getting some aspirin. He has another headache."

It took three long strides to reach his chair. I squatted next to it, gripping the arm, and tried to keep my voice from trembling. "I don't want Aldo to overhear us, so keep your voice low. I know where the artifact is."

For an instant I thought he was going to jump out of his chair. He poked his face almost into mine and hissed, "You found it? You've got it?"

"I know where it is," I said, "and in a few minutes I'm going to get it and bring it to you."

His gaze darted toward the stairs and back to me, then back and forth again. I glanced at the stairs, too, but Aldo wasn't in sight. "Why don't you just tell me where it is and I'll get it?" he asked.

"Because you need to stay here with Aldo. You're protecting us, and besides, we can't take the chance that he'll get his hands on it."

"Yeah," he said. "Right." Then he squinted suspiciously at me. "How'd you find it?"

"Do you want me to get it or not?" I asked.

"You're going to bring it to me?"

"That's what you told me to do, isn't it?"

"How long is this going to take?"

"Maybe twenty minutes."

He scowled. "Come on. No one could have taken it out of the house."

"Someone did," I said.

"Do you know who that person was?"

I nodded. "Yes, I do. I'll tell you later. Will you wait here? Shall I get it?" By this time I hoped that Pete had the others in tow and they were making their way through the woods toward the motorboat.

It was obvious that Kurt was trying out every option that came to his mind. He could force me to take him to where the artifact was hidden, but he wasn't sure what Madelyn or Benita would do. He could call to Aldo, but that would give their connection away. As far as he knew, I had believed the story he'd given me. Here I was, offering to bring him the artifact. He suddenly shrugged and said, "Go ahead. Get it. I'll wait here for you."

I raced out of the house and down to the pier, where I kicked off my sandals and dived into the water. There was no time to change into a bathing suit, but my shorts and T-shirt were easy to swim in.

I was glad for the swimming lessons, glad for the practice over the summers at the Y pool and at Galveston beach. I kept a strong, steady stroke until I reached the promontory. The tide was coming in, just as it had been before, so I dived deeply through the arch and twisted to enter the cave before I surfaced. I scrambled onto the ledge, scraping my knees and one elbow, and hopped over the rough limestone to the niche where the towel was still wedged.

With shaking fingers I unfolded the towel and removed the topaz, which was even more spectacular than I had remembered. Even in the dim light of the cave it glowed with a blue fire. The golden monkey hovered over it, his eyes reflecting sparks from the stone. I felt as though he were staring directly at me.

It took only a minute to slip the ribbon over my head and tuck the topaz down inside my T-shirt, wedging it under my bra. But the monkey's sharp little paws dug painfully into my skin.

I picked up the towel. Maybe I should replace it, just to mark the spot. The police would come to investigate the murders and, even though the artifact would be well on its way to Peru, I'd need to show them where it had been hidden. I folded the towel and tucked it back into the niche.

I walked to the edge of the ledge, ready to slide back into the water, hoping with all my heart that Pete and the motorboat would show up soon.

But the water beneath me exploded as Kurt shot through, his big hands grabbing the ledge. He pulled himself up, grinning, shouting at me, as I stumbled back.

"Give it to me!" he yelled. "Give me the artifact!"

CHAPTER

~~~~~~~~~~~~~~~~~~~~~~~~~~~

14

It was like trying to wake from a bad dream when you want to scream but you can't. I opened my mouth but only some croaking noises came out.

"Where is it?" he demanded.

I pointed at the towel.

Greedily, Kurt stumbled over the ledge and shoved a fist into the niche, grabbing for the towel. He was no longer between me and the entrance to the cave.

I ran and jumped, blindly. A sharp pain stabbed up my leg as my ankle scraped the rock, but I didn't let it stop me. Down I went, swooping through the arch as though I were as fast and sleek as a fish. I didn't look back. I didn't dare to. I surfaced, swimming with all my might. I could hear Kurt splashing behind me. He wasn't far away.

No boat. Not even the sound of the boat. Pete hadn't been able to start it. He wouldn't come. I was out here with Kurt, who was bigger and stronger than I was. There'd be no contest.

From the corner of one eye I caught a movement and automatically dived just as he lunged for me, leaving him off balance and flailing on the surface. The sea wasn't deep this close to land, and I could see a cluster of conchs among the wavering sea plants below me. I came up behind Kurt, pulled on one leg to jerk him under, and twisted away.

When I came up for air I was about five feet from Kurt. He was coughing and spitting. Luckily, my maneuver had caused him to gulp a mouthful of salt water.

I dived again, this time with a purpose. I picked up one of the conchs, looked up to see Kurt's position, and shot up behind him.

Raising the conch high in the air, I banged it down on the back of Kurt's head. He went limp and slid under the water. I dropped the conch, pulled Kurt's head up so that he could breathe, and treaded water.

I was so thankful when I heard the boat's motor that I shouted and whooped. Around the promontory it came. Pete was steering and searching.

Madelyn, who was on her feet, too, screamed, "Andrea!" She picked up a thermos and held it over her head like a weapon.

"It's all right!" I shouted. I realized that they couldn't hear me, but I couldn't let Kurt get bashed again, so I tried to use sign language. I felt Kurt stirring. I was glad he was going to regain consciousness, but I didn't want to be this close to him when he did. "Hurry!" I yelled.

Pete slowed to a stop, and the boat slid close to me.

"Kurt's coming to," I said as Kurt began to move his head up and down and mumble.

"Don't worry," Pete said. He dropped the ladder over the side.

I grabbed it with my free hand, but Kurt suddenly reached out and grabbed it too.

"Uh-uh," Pete said. He leaned over the side and poked a small handgun into Kurt's face. "You want to swim to shore," he said. "There's a nice little beach just a few yards away."

Kurt looked at the gun. "I know," Pete said. "It's yours. I found it in the boat. Dirty trick, wasn't it? Now, swim."

Madelyn still held that threatening thermos in the air, and Ellison had picked up some kind of a tool. Benita sat with her hands over her eyes, but I hadn't expected anything very helpful from her, so it wasn't a surprise. Kurt stared at each of them in turn. It didn't take long for him to make up his mind. He struck out for shore, and I scrambled aboard.

"Did you get it?" Pete asked.

"Yes," I said.

"Could I see it?"

I looked at the gun, which he still held. He looked at it, too, as though he'd forgotten it was there, and quietly handed it to me.

Laughing with relief, I put the gun down on the bench beside me. "Here's the artifact," I said. I tugged on the ribbon, and the artifact slid from the neckline of my shirt. In the bright sunlight it was like a grand finale of fireworks, shooting glorious sparks of blue and gold.

Pete just stared at it, for once without words.

Kurt had reached the beach. He angrily yelled something at us, but I had no idea what it was, because Benita had picked up the gun, pointing it at each of us in turn. "Give that to me," she said in a strange, tight voice.

"What are you doing, Benita? Put down that gun immediately. You don't know what to do with a gun!" Madelyn demanded.

"Oh, yes I do," Benita said, and the gun shook in her hands. I wished she wasn't pointing it at us. "You don't know how badly I need that artifact."

"Enough to kill us for it?" My voice trembled too. I'd never been so frightened. It was horrifying to see that gun pointed at us and know that she might pull the trigger.

"Be quiet," she demanded.

Aunt Madelyn tried to move in front of me, but Benita shoved her aside with such force that Madelyn fell against the seat.

"Benita!" Madelyn said, and rubbed her arm, wincing at the pain. "This is foolish! You can't just take possession of the artifact. How will you manage to keep us all at gunpoint all the way to Grand Bahama Island?"

"I won't have to try," Benita said. "You can all swim to shore, just as Kurt did. I know how to pilot this boat myself. But first . . ." She waved the gun in my direction. "Give me the artifact, Andrea."

I shook my head. "No. It's not fair."

"Fair?" she screeched. "Don't talk nonsense! You're old enough to know that life isn't fair. You heard me! Give me that artifact!"

"I won't do it," I told her.

She raised the gun and pointed it at my head. I squeezed my eyes shut and waited.

CHAPTER

~~~~~~~~~~~~~~~~~~~~~~~~

15

"That's enough," I heard Pete saying. "She's not going to hurt you, Andy."

I opened my eyes to see him reach out and grab the barrel of the gun.

Benita screeched in panic and pulled the trigger, but there was only an empty click.

"I took the bullets out," Pete explained to me. "Loaded guns make me nervous." He examined it. "We don't need this thing. Let's get rid of it," he said, and pitched it into the ocean.

Benita flopped to the bench and sobbed.

"What should we do with Mrs. Robley?" Ellison asked.

Madelyn's expression softened, and she put an arm around Benita's shoulders. "We'll take her home," she said.

"Aunt Madelyn," I murmured, and when she looked up—a question in her eyes—I grinned at her. "I love you," I said.

Pete turned up the motor with a roar, and off we went into a sweeping circle.

Benita staggered down the steps into the cabin, still crying and tugging Madelyn with her. Ellison stretched out on the cushions on one side and closed his eyes. I stood close to Pete, my arms around him—for support of course. The boat bounced over the water, and I lifted my face to catch the sting of salt spray.

"As long as we're going to Freeport, I'll pick up my boat and tow it in," he said.

"When we're in Freeport will you help me contact the authorities in Peru?"

"I've got a much better idea," Pete said. "How about if I drop our passengers off in Freeport and take you straight to Peru?" he asked.

"A nice thought, but impractical," I said.

"It will be hard to say good-bye."

"We don't have to for a while, not if you don't mind hanging around Palm Beach for the next couple of weeks. I'll even buy you a tie."

He smiled. "You want to see me?"

"Do you think I should roll with the punches and accept things the way they are and admit that life isn't fair? In other words, should I grow up?" I asked him.

"I don't believe that's what growing up means," he said. "Do you?"

"No," I said. "I don't."

"Good," Pete said. "Because I like you the way you are, and I hope you'll stay that way all your life."

The boat made a wide swing as Pete let go of the

wheel and planted a kiss somewhere near my chin. "Let's compromise," he said. "If you don't want Peru, how about the Panama Canal? Acapulco? Puerto Vallarta?"

"Will you let me steer the boat?"

"Sure," he said. "Cozumel? Cancun? Key West?"

"I mean now."

"Oh," he said. "Do you think you'll know the way?"

I laughed. "Yes," I said. "I'm sure of it."